About the Author

Dave Meakin is a first-time author who has had an interest in writing fiction since he was young. In 2012 he went on his first coach holiday to the seaside resort of Blackpool, where he picked up a few interesting tales. Over the course of the next eight years, he went on other coach holidays to resorts around the UK picking up more tales to add to the others he had remembered and compiled them into a fictional story. Dave was born in 1978 and has lived all of his life in the small Leicestershire village of Ibstock.

Coach Holiday

Dave Meakin

Coach Holiday

Olympia Publishers
London

www.olympiapublishers.com
OLYMPIA PAPERBACK EDITION

A CIP catalogue record for this title is
available from the British Library.

ISBN: **978-1-78830-963-9**

This is a work of fiction.
Names, characters, places and incidents originate from the writer's
imagination. Any resemblance to actual persons, living or dead, is
purely coincidental.

First Published in 2021

Olympia Publishers
Tallis House
2 Tallis Street
London
EC4Y 0AB

Printed in Great Britain

Prologue

The holiday brochure for the coach company was certainly informative. The cover showed one of its sparkling new coaches parked diagonally across a car park somewhere in the glorious sunshine with its smartly dressed (but slightly overweight) driver standing proudly by the door. On the side of the gold-painted coach read the coach company name 'Golden Trip Coaches' in red lettering followed by a picture of an open treasure chest and a comet-like tail shooting out of it as if to indicate that the company name is shooting out of the treasure chest. Standing at the other end of the coach so as not to obscure the coach company's name on the side of the vehicle were presumably five of the company's satisfied customers. All of them were pensioners and all were smiling and wearing what passed for holiday clothes for the people of their generation. Two of them were men and three were women and at first I thought maybe they were some kind of old-age gang-bang party but then I figured that Golden Trip Coaches wouldn't advertise such things and these seemingly innocent and happy customers were likely two married couples and the widow spending her late husband's inheritance on a coach holiday! Both men were wearing light coloured breezy shirts and beige trousers while the women wore white sunhats and either long floral-patterned dresses or a floral-patterned shirt and white trousers. All five of them looked in the peak of health and were dressed for a nice summer's day.

Inside the brochure was the usual stuff about how amazing the coach company was and how happy their customers were along with more pictures of happy customers over the age of sixty-five and more overweight drivers as well as the obligatory picture of a young female receptionist manning telephone calls via a headset and a large smile on her face as she looked at the camera. Golden Trip Coaches apparently prided themselves on providing people with amazing holidays which included at least two day-trips thrown into the package. Nothing so far deterred me from booking a holiday with the company despite the obvious fact that I would most likely stick out on the coach like a sore thumb due to me being over thirty years younger than everybody else on the coach! After the past few months at work, I've had recently, I needed a break but one in the sunny climes of Spain or Portugal wasn't within my budget so it had to be a British seaside holiday by a coach firm whom people have told me about over the years but I've never been on holiday with. I turned over to the first page of holidays in the brochure and read what Golden Trip Coaches had to say about its first listed holiday.

Claptout-by-the-Sea was a holiday resort on the other side of the country to where I lived. I'd never been there in my life but have seemingly always wanted to go there. I read what the brochure had to say about the holiday and it seemed like such a nice place. Golden sands, blue sea, lovely green gardens and lots of shops and attractions to see which piqued my interest but were likely over embellished accounts of what the resort really looked like. Attractions such as amusement arcades and large aquariums interested me and Claptout-by-the-Sea offered all of these. The resort also had two piers with attractions on each of them which furthered my interest.

Golden Trip Holidays also threw in three day trips in their seven-day holiday to Clapout-by-the-Sea which was a bonus as far as I was concerned. The first was a full day to the nearby 'ye-olde' village of Claptrap which, if I recall from a school trip many, many years ago had very little to offer other than a medieval castle, a few stone-built walls, and many fields. Still, Claptrap might be a fun place to visit as I hadn't been there for over twenty years and since then, the tourism trade has picked up and there would likely be many gift shops in the place where people such as me could pick up a handful of fridge magnets and cheap-looking pens and pencils with the village name printed on them! When I had last visited Claptrap, it was visited only by a few Americans who seemed to enjoy the sights of 'Englund' most likely because their own country was either packed full of skyscrapers or packed full of cowboys on horses shouting 'yee-haa' down your ear every thirty seconds!

The second day trip took in two places. First, we would travel to the market town of Cowshit (the town is pronounced as Cows-hit for anybody not familiar with the area) and then we would finish the day trip by travelling onwards to the small seaside resort of Boggy Sands which used to be known for its involvement with the family seaside company Bunton's Holidays who had a series of chalets and caravans in an area nearby but ultimately went bust a few years ago. The Bunton's Holidays area still exists in Boggy Sands but its chalets and caravans are now derelict and falling apart and have been lovingly touched up by graffiti artists while their once ocean-blue swimming pools are now either empty or green with a combination of algae and urine. The monorail train that once served the whole of the Bunton's resort is now rusted and is currently lying on its side in the middle of a small kids' football pitch following its collapse off the overhead rails a few years ago when the rails went rusty and fell apart. How do I know this? Simple. I was there on an earlier coach holiday when it happened!

The third and final day trip is to the university city of Scruff which is about as interesting as watching paint dry! The place is nothing but one giant university campus where all of the inhabitants are under the age of thirty and when they're not doing chalk drawings on the pavements they're doing some other form of pavement desecration such as spitting! I went there a few years ago and I managed to pass myself off as a student at the time. An elderly woman even came up to me during the day trip and asked me which subjects I was taking which I politely answered back in the form of sarcasm. 'I'm learning pornography,' I replied at which point she showed her lack of knowledge on the subject by smiling and saying 'well, I hope you do well and study hard young man!' At the time I was a clean-shaven twenty-five-year-old, but now, twelve years on I'll most likely have the genuine university students coming up to me and sneering at me before uttering the words 'bloody tourist' under their breath before unfurling their banners and starting a protest march based on something as trivial as hedgehogs crossing the road!

Claptout-by-the-Sea looked to be an excellent holiday and one I'm seriously tempted to go on. The coach will no doubt be full of people who would fit in more in a retirement home but who cares! Even if the holiday was bad, it would still be a holiday and I would take memories away from it.

The following day I walked the short distance to my local travel agent to make the booking. (I could have phoned up Golden Trip Coaches directly or even booked the holiday through their website but I doubt anybody else on the coach would have done that so why should I?). The travel agents in my home town were the usual bog-standard travel agents that seemed to be staffed by young and middle-aged women who dressed like they were about to go to a fancy dress party dressed as air hostesses. The carpet on the floor at first glance looked like a standard grey carpet with odd patterns on it but upon closer inspection (I bent down to tie my shoelaces) I noticed that the carpet was adorned with the logo of the travel agent in question. This got me thinking. I wonder if I could have a carpet put in my house with my face printed all over it or something else that symbolised me?

I walked over to one of the desks brandishing a copy of the Golden Trip Coaches brochure and sat down. I opened the brochure up on the page which advertised Claptout-by-the-Sea and said almost proudly 'I would like to book this holiday please.'

The young woman sitting behind the desk stopped filing her nails with what appeared to be a Swiss Army knife and looked at me. 'The Golden Trip Coaches advisor is on the far end desk,' she said as she chewed some gum 'I only deal with foreign holidays!' With that she continued to file her nails. I stood up and then sat back down at the desk indicated by the other travel agent and smiled at the considerably older woman behind the desk. Attached to the side of her computer screen by Blu-tack was a piece of printed paper with the Golden Trip Coaches logo on it and the words 'Official Holiday Rep' in black lettering underneath. I went through the same procedure again as I did with the first woman and this time I received a more polite response.

'So you want to go to Claptout-by-the-Sea do you,' said the woman who looked like she was in her fifties.

'I do indeed,' I replied.

'Have you ever been there before?' came the next question.

'Never. I have been told it's a good place to go though.'

'It is a good place in the summer months — nothing but sunshine.'

'That's one of the reasons why I want to go there.'

'Golden Trip Coaches also throw in a few day trips. I'm assured they're very good day trips.'

'You can't beat a good city break.'

The patter went on for almost ten minutes before any part of the holiday was even booked but finally it was and I paid for it in full using my bank card. All I had to do now was to book the week off work.

My boss laughed at me on the Monday morning when I turned up for work and asked him for a week off. As I walked into his office I was immediately assaulted by his choice of radio station ringing out from a stereo in his office. It was a commercial station called Jewel 666 that tended to only play the same twenty songs twice a day every day. Fortunately, it was only on the radio in his office and rarely did any of the workers hear it for any length of time. If they did, however, the factory would no doubt have a high suicide rate!

'You want to go on a coach holiday?' he chuckled, 'I've heard of people wanting to return to their childhood but you appear to want to live the life of an old biddy long before you've even retired!'

'I like British seaside resorts,' I replied, 'there's something about them that you don't find in foreign holidays.'

'Absolutely true,' said my boss with a chuckle before listing things that you only find in British seaside holidays. 'Filthy water, seaweed and empty drinks cans on the beach, seagull shit on the pavement and also occasionally on your clothes — yep you certainly get something different on a British coach holiday!'

'There are some good things about a British holiday.' I retorted.

'Like what?' he asked.

'Nice weather and...' I tried to think of some other reasons but couldn't off the top of my head. My boss leaned back in his chair which made a squeak as it did so as if to plead for the slightly overweight manager to stand up.

'Nice weather?' he said quizzically, 'you get a lot of rain in some parts. I went to a holiday resort in July last year and it snowed on one of the days! It then pissed down with rain for the next two days which cleared away the snow only for the snow to return on the fourth day. We also had terrible wind throughout the holiday.'

'You shouldn't have had too many curries then!' I joked.

'I mean terrible wind as in bad weather,' he said not amused by my joke. 'Although we did take in a curry house while we were there. There's a lovely restaurant empire in some holiday resorts run by this bloke called Josh Rogan. His restaurants do some lovely vindaloo's.'

'So can I have the week off work?' I asked finally.

The man sighed and nodded. 'There's not much work going on here anyway at the moment. I doubt this place will still be open this time next year.'

'So, I can have it off then?'

'Yes — but only if you bring me back a fridge magnet and a stick of rock!'

I finished work that day with happiness. Everything was now sorted and I was looking forward to going on my coach holiday with Golden Trip Coaches.

Chapter 1
The Journey

To say that I was excited was an understatement. It was the morning of my holiday to Claptout-by-the Sea and I had been waiting for this moment for a long while. I stood at the pick-up point for the feeder coach to take me to the service station where I would join the main holiday coach in what I considered to be appropriate holiday clothes. I was wearing a blue and white striped short-sleeved shirt, dark trousers and white trainers as I waited patiently with my large blue suitcase packed full of clothing for a full week and also a small black hand luggage bag which was largely empty at the moment but would likely be full with various trinkets when I returned.

As I waited for the feeder coach to arrive I surveyed my surroundings. I was waiting at a bus stop that was like a book written by yobs as it was covered in graffiti. Out of boredom I read some of the scrawls and chuckled. 'I was 'ere last week but I'm not 'ere now!' was one of the poetic scribblings. I then thought about that for a moment. If the author wasn't 'ere now how did he manage to write this? 'Barry luvs Jessica and Kirsty but also luvs Gemma' was another one which sounded much like some kind of admission to a gang-bang! 'The KFC kid is in da house' wrote another luminary. Assuming that 'da house' was the nearest KFC restaurant (assuming also that the letters KFC was the acronym for a popular fast food restaurant) I imagined that this 'kid' walked proudly through the doors of the restaurant on a Saturday morning, thrust his arms into the air and hollered his arrival as other people were eating! The nearest such restaurant however was a good fifteen miles away however so what that was doing written on a bus stop in a town that has seen better days was beyond me!

Near to the bus stop was a string of shops including a large supermarket. 'Mega Mart' had been in the town for many years and had gone under many different names. I remember it being built on top of a house that was said to be haunted. The house caught fire one day and the shop owners brought the site less than a week later. Locals claimed it was the ghost that set fire to the fire but I was adamant that the fire was caused by the people who wanted to build the shop there! After the shop had been built some locals claimed that they had seen the ghost do some shopping there which always made me chuckle! Thoughts of a ghost wheeling a wonky shopping trolley around the store sticking cans of lager into the trolley before arriving at the tobacconist counter and asking for twenty fags went through my mind every time I heard that story! 'Mega Mart' was busy this morning and I observed several families and pensioners leaving the store and packing the boots of their car with their weekly shopping. One young man who appeared to have got his dress sense from Sid Vicious walked out of the store with a six-pack of lager in one hand and his car keys in the other. He opened the door of his car, sat in and opened a can of lager before drinking some of it and driving off!

The feeder coach was a full twenty minutes late but that didn't deter me. It did however cause a few minor complaints from the five other people waiting for the same feeder coach who wanted to reach their holiday resort as soon as possible. Before the coach arrived I got talking to one or two of the other holidaymakers waiting who were all over the age of fifty.

'So, where are you going?' I asked one of them — a woman in her fifties who, like me was seemingly holidaying alone.

'I'm going to Muddy Beach,' she replied, 'it's always good at this time of year.' Muddy Beach was a holiday resort I preferred to stay away from. It was one of the British holiday resorts where there was absolutely nothing to do. There was a beach of sorts there but it was usually waterlogged according to reports and it had an amazing amount of seafront gardens and high street shops but nothing at all that shouted out holiday to me.

'What do you plan to do there?' was my next question. I was expecting a question along the lines of, 'go out and enjoy myself' but what I got was something different.

'I plan to stay in my hotel room for much of the holiday!' she replied, 'I come to holiday to relax and that's what I'm going to do!' I was going to relax as well but I was also going to see the sights and catch the invigorating sea air. Sitting in my hotel room all week wasn't something I was planning to do unless it rained every single day for the entire duration of the holiday. If I wanted to sit down and stare at a wall inside a room for a whole week I wouldn't have paid over £200 for this holiday and would have chosen to sit in my armchair at home watching the lounge room wallpaper!

When the feeder coach arrived my case was put into the luggage compartment and I boarded the vehicle with my hand luggage and sat down. I had expected a Golden Trip Coaches bus but instead we got a minibus from a local taxi company that had seen better days. The minibus set off and for the next half hour I suffered a back-aching ride from a vehicle that clearly needed an MOT! Surprisingly the other passengers didn't complain about the bumpy ride. I put this down to the possible fact that it reminded them of the days from their childhood where they travelled around in horse-drawn carriages along cobbled streets!

Crappy Services was an exclusively coach holiday orientated service station. Situated on the outskirts of a town called Lower Itches it boasted several known fast food kiosks and a few more that I had never heard of before. This wasn't the first time I had been here because the holiday coach I took last year also picked up from here. The minibus arrived at the service station about an hour before the main tour coach was due to arrive and I took this time to review my surroundings. Several Golden Trip coaches were parked up in the station in bays that were clearly designed for coach use but none of them were for any of the minibus passengers. I watched as my case was wheeled by a porter to an area where the Claptout-by-the-Sea coach would park up before walking into the service station for a bite to eat. I approached a canteen that served traditional British breakfasts and ordered one such meal which they described as, 'A Big British Breakfast for a Big British person!' I had a slight paunch to my figure but I wouldn't exactly describe myself as a, 'Big British person'. I sat at a table and the breakfast was handed to me on a cracked white plate. Burnt sausages and bacon complimented a small portion of scrambled eggs that looked as if they had been cooked yesterday and a few mushrooms that were dripping in water as well as cold fried tomatoes wasn't exactly worth the five pounds I had paid for the meal but I couldn't complain. It was either this meal or starve until I reached the hotel at the holiday resort.

After I had eaten the unappetising meal I stepped into a newsagents and perused the magazines. I'm a fan of fast cars and motor racing and there were a few of these magazines that I could choose from. As I picked up one such magazine an elderly couple stood next to me. These two were most likely going on holiday as well and I assumed that they were one of the Muddy Beach holidaymakers. The elderly man looked at me and gave me a sneer before picking up a gardening magazine and looking through it. As I looked through my choice of magazine I watched the couple out of the corner of my eye like some kind of comic book spy. They had a gardening magazine each and were seemingly comparing tips as they each pointed out articles in their respective magazines and nodded in appreciation. I decided to purchase my magazine as well as a bottle of fizzy orange with the newsagents own brand name on it before leaving. As I did so I looked back at the elderly couple who were still reading the magazines. Just before I averted my gaze the man gave me one more nasty looking sneer.

Like the public bus service that ran in my home village five Golden Trip coaches pulled into Crappy Services at the same time after I had been waiting countless minutes for just one of them! The golden colour of each coach acted as some sort of sun reflector and the sunshine that bore down on everybody waiting hit the coach panels and then bounced off into my eyes and made them run. All five coaches were driven by overweight drivers and I watched from a distance as one of the drivers put mine and other people's luggage onto the coach. A woman wearing a hi-visibility vest then called out through a loudhailer. 'Can all people travelling to Claptout-by-the-Sea please board coach number four.' Me and about forty others —

mostly people over the age of sixty — boarded the coach and sat in our respective seats. Soon after I sat down however I noticed the elderly couple from the newsagents board the coach. A third sneer was delivered to me by the man as he walked past me and I noticed that they hadn't got any magazines in their hands. I suppose they could have brought one and put it in the handbag that the woman was carrying but if it wasn't in there then they had spent about twenty minutes reading magazines in the newsagents without any intention to buy them!

After everybody was seated the coach rumbled and I thought that the engine had started but no, it was the overweight coach driver getting back onto the bus! He then started the engine and the vehicle rumbled into life before he walked down the aisle of the coach and counted every passenger. Once he was satisfied that everybody was on board he sat in the driver's seat and closed the door to the coach.

Moments later the coach pulled out of the service station and started on its way towards the peaceful holiday resort of Claptout-by-the-Sea. Just as I was about to relax in my seat I heard a deep guttural belch. I looked around and noticed that it was the driver! He had turned on the tannoy system on the coach seemingly just to let all of his passengers know that he had already eaten! The driver then spoke.

'Hello everybody,' he said in a cheery but monotonous voice, 'my name is Paul and I'd like to wish you all a very good morning on behalf of Golden Trip Holidays. I'll be your driver for the following week and I'll be taking you on three separate day trips. The first we'll be going to the lovely picturesque village of Claptrap where life slows down to a crawl. En route to Claptrap we'll be travelling through several pretty little villages that you will enjoy the sight of.' (the term 'travelling through several pretty little villages' usually meant the coach driving down tight single lane roads that threatened to drive over somebody's front garden because the vehicle was too wide for the road before we drive past rows and rows of thatched houses!)

'On our second day trip' continued the coach driver, 'we will travel downhill until we're deep in Cowshit which is another lovely village where you can marvel at lots of thatched houses and lovely country roads before travelling onwards to the quaint seaside resort of Boggy Sands where you can walk amongst all of the high street shops there. Finally, on our third and final day trip we will visit the university city of Scruff where all of the students there don't like to be known as students but rather as 'Scruffs'!' The driver then ended with another belch and turned off the tannoy.

I reclined the seat I was sitting in and was just about to relax when I suddenly heard a young male voice shout, 'Ha ha, take that you red candy. How do you like the taste of a Color Bomb?' I looked backwards to a seat not far behind my own and saw a young man around the same age as me playing a well-known puzzle game on his mobile. I thought I was the only person under retirement age on this coach but it seemed like I wasn't. After he signalled that his game was over (by shouting the word 'bollocks' no less) he went quiet. I reclined once more and fell into an uneasy sleep.

The dream I had was bizarre. It started by me getting on the coach at the graffiti covered bus stop rather than the service station with the driver being the lager lout from the Mega Mart store. As the coach raced along the roads like a Formula One car the driver finished his third can of lager. He then belched through the tannoy followed by the words, 'I wholly recommend this brand of lager!' The coach then turned on its side and skidded into Crappy Services like a skateboard with no wheels! The lager lout got out of the coach through the windows as did all of the passengers before we boarded another coach driven by the real coach driver. He was more careful on the roads but he did take us on a journey through several 'quaint little villages'. After travelling the wrong way down several one-way streets we arrived at Claptout-by-the Sea only to discover that it was the twin of Boggy Sands! The entire holiday then passed by in a blur where I spent much of my time wading through the muddy beach in a pair of wellington boots!

I was awoken about an hour later by the sound of the coach engine lowering its tone as if getting ready to stop. I looked out of the window and noticed that we were driving into another service station. Whereas the previous one was a special coach holiday service station this one we were pulling into was a standard one designed for any type of vehicle. I waited for the coach driver to belch before explaining to us why we were stopping here but he didn't. He just went straight into the explanation which, to me, seemed akin to the railway station announcer explaining the delay of your train over the tannoy without starting it with the familiar 'ding dong' ring that normally preceded it.

'We will be stopping here for forty-five minutes,' explained the driver, 'before carrying on to Claptout-by-the-Sea. Make sure you are back on the coach at the correct time.' He then opened up the main door of the coach and also the side fire exit door which was very helpful to me because the aisle of the coach was now suddenly packed with elderly men and women slowly departing the coach. If I used the main door it would probably take me about forty-five minutes to exit the coach!

This service station was clearly smaller than the main one we were all picked up from. As usual it housed a few well known takeaway kiosks as well as a few fast food kiosks that I liked to call 'posh eateries' solely because they only seemed to exist in proper shop form in posh areas of cities and towns and displayed menus with prices that you could only pay by credit card! I walked into the service station, picked up a pack of sandwiches and a bottle of cola from a convenience store I found within and then walked back out to sit on a low fence outside surrounding a small garden feature.

The coach pulled off again on time and we were now on the final leg of the journey towards the holiday resort. My excitement on the thought of getting closer and closer to the seaside rose but then dropped again when I heard the young man behind me shout, 'Take that, you stupid blue candy!' After an hour on the road we reached Claptout-by-the-Sea. We drove through a few side streets before turning onto the promenade. On one side was the beach and sea along with the two piers and on the other side were a few side roads full of takeaway shops and gift shops. My interest piqued when I noticed that one such shop was called 'Fridge Magnet Paradise'. That was certainly one shop I would be visiting at some point in the holiday! The same shop also sold sticks of rock and underneath the shop name written in smaller letters was '(and we also sell sticks of rock)'! I'd certainly be buying a few sticks of rock whilst I was here but it wouldn't be as high up on my list as fridge magnets! We also drove past a couple of small crazy golf attractions and also a kids play area that looked like it had seen better days.

The coach eventually stopped at a hotel a few minutes away from the main tourist area of Claptout-by-the-Sea. The hotel was a large Georgian building that looked like its heyday was far in the past but that was of no concern to me. I couldn't really care less if the hotel was a wreck because I would be spending more time out of the hotel than in it. The hotel was called 'The Claptout Hotel' and had been recently painted in a shade of white that looked like it had been slapped on by a load of amateurs. The hotel name was plastered in large plastic blue lettering just above the front entrance and was slightly spattered with the paint from the building. The coach driver forgot to belch into the tannoy again as he told all of the passengers to stay on the coach until all of the luggage had been unloaded and the hotel manager had boarded the coach to welcome us all here.

The hotel manager was actually a manageress and she beamed us all a warm smile before speaking.

'Hello everybody,' she smiled. 'My name is Janet and I'm the manageress of The Claptout Hotel. All of the staff at the hotel wish to welcome you to Claptout-by-the-Sea and I hope you all have a lovely time here and also a comfortable stay at the hotel.' She then went through a series of explanations detailing which floor of the hotel the bar was, where all of the lifts and fire exits were and also the fact that bingo is played in the bar every night. She then welcomed us all to Claptout-by-the-Sea once more and stepped off the coach and promptly tripped over one of the suitcases that had recently been offloaded from the coach!

Chapter 2
The First Day

The Claptout Hotel was typical of any two-star hotel I had stayed in before. The reception area was clean and tidy and looked quite neat while the hotel staff were largely good-looking females with foreign accents. As I waited for my key to the hotel room I observed a couple of glass cabinets against one of the walls in reception. One of them displayed pens, pencils and even fridge magnets displaying the hotel name while the other displayed various items of jewellery. I might be interested in the pens and pencils and would certainly pick up a fridge magnet but the jewellery wasn't something I'd buy. All of it looked like women's jewellery and ranged from bracelets and necklaces to rings and brooches and the reason I wouldn't ever be buying anything like that was because I had no woman in my life at the moment. My last girlfriend ditched me for my best mate about five or six years ago and I think our parting was why I started going on these coach holidays in the first place. I needed a break away from reality and a coach holiday was just cheap enough to satisfy these demands.

I picked up the key to my hotel room eventually and walked up three flights of steps to the room. I could have taken the lift but that would have meant I had to wait at the back of a queue of slow moving pensioners all filing into the lift at the same time. After looking around for my room for at least a good five minutes I eventually found it. The directions the receptionist had given me in her sexy Russian accent didn't help and I had to use my own knowledge of looking for hard-to-find hotel rooms in coach holiday hotels to find it. On a previous coach holiday it took me over half an hour to find my hotel room due to the fact that the receptionist had initially directed me onto the wrong floor and then when I took the lift up to the correct floor it had dropped me off at the opposite end of the hotel. After walking past a door several times that looked like a store cupboard I went through the door and found my hotel door beyond it!

Room 235 was the room I had been given and when I opened the door I had a quick look around before entering as if I was expecting some kind of TV prankster to jump out of the wardrobe and surprise me. The room passed my own low standards of two-star hotel rooms and as I inspected the room in closer detail I ticked off all of the things I expected to find in the room from a mental note in my head:

Excellent view of somebody's back yard with overflowing dustbins out of the window? Yep, this had it!

Cigarette burn hole in the net curtains? I wasn't disappointed!

Curious brown mark on the wall next to the en-suite bathroom door? I was sort of pleased to find one!

Cigarette burn marks on the window and fag ends on the sill outside? Tradition always pleases me!

Solitary strand of curly hair (possibly pubic) on the toilet seat? Nothing ever changes!

All in all, the room had everything I was expecting it to have! As I waited for my luggage to be brought up to my room by one of the porters I made myself a cup of tea using the small cheap-looking plastic kettle (that I had to fill with water from the bathroom tap) and the individually wrapped teabags and small cartons of milk provided. As I was just about to finish my cuppa there was a knock on the door. I opened it and found my suitcase sitting outside. I carried it into my room and quickly unpacked my clothes into the various drawers (some of which were either stiff or broken) before falling down on my bed for a quick lie down. The bed squeaked as I collapsed onto it and then the legs at the bottom of the bed collapsed in sympathy! I stood up and looked underneath the bottom of the bed only to discover that the legs were broken and had been for some time. I hastily repaired the legs by standing them up domino fashion so that the base of the bed rested on top of them uneasily and promised to report it to the receptionist later on before lying down on the bed once more.

After a quick snooze I got up and decided to take a look around Claptout-by-the-Sea. According to a small card that was given to me along with my room key, dinner in the hotel restaurant wasn't served until 7pm (the same card also assured me that breakfast was at 8.30am every morning) so I had a few hours to myself. I exited the hotel and was just about to walk down the road leading to the beach when I noticed the young man from the coach who had spent some of the journey playing mobile games. I walked up to him and introduced myself to the cigarette smoking fellow guest.

'Hi, I'm Dave,' I said as I held out my hand. 'I saw you on the coach earlier.'

'Jack,' replied the young man as he shook my hand. 'Aren't you a bit too young to be going on coach holidays like this?' I laughed and nodded. 'I suppose I am,' I replied, 'and you are as well. These kind of holidays seem to only bring out the pensioners! What brings you here?'

Jack stubbed out his current cigarette and promptly lit up another one and ushered me to walk along the road with him. 'I like the good old fashioned British holiday resort,' he revealed. 'There's something nice and relaxing about them that you just don't find in those foreign holidays. The foreigners can keep their clean white sand beaches and tropical heat I'd rather have a wet seaweed covered British beach and warm — but not hot — weather any day.'

'I'm the same,' I said in agreement. 'I'd rather buy a fridge magnet than a cocktail poured into a coconut shell any day of the week!'

Jack laughed and we continued our walk towards the beach.

After picking up a couple of fridge magnets for me and an ice cream for Jack I pressed him if he had been here before.

'I came here last year with Golden Trip Coaches,' he admitted, 'the hotel is still the same shit hole it was last year! They've even put me in the same room!'

'How do you know?' I asked.

'Last year I made a little mark with a red felt tip pen above the wardrobe on the wallpaper — a mark that looked like dripping blood! And guess what? It's still there!'

'What about the meals and the evening entertainment?' I asked.

'The meals are bog standard stuff — or should I say dog standard! I swear the meat pie I ate on one of the days last year was made by Pedigree! The evening entertainment is also shit! They always start off with a game of bingo — and let me tell you — the oldies do not like it when somebody my age beats them! One couple gave me ever such a nasty look when I won one of the games last year. It was like I'd committed a murder or something! The entertainment is also dire but it's made even more terrible by the oldies who are tapping their toes — and most likely their Zimmer frames at the fifty-year-old music the guest singers always do.'

I was interested. 'What happens then?' I said.

'Last year one of the guest singers did a collection of hits by Val Doonican, Des O'Connor and the like and when he'd finished he asked if anybody would like to request a song. The singer claimed he could sing over five hundred different songs and so I was going to request something from Black Sabbath or Def Leppard but the oldies beat me to it and they asked for more Val Doonican with a bit of Roger Whittaker and Slim Whitman thrown in for variety! I left the hotel bar in disgust and had a few drinks in a lovely bar which does live music. If you're interested you could join me tonight.' Jack then showed me the bar in question as we walked past it and I said that I'd give it a go but I wanted to sample this so-called bad hotel entertainment tonight first.

A third cigarette was swiftly smoked by my fellow holiday guest as he found my insistence of seeing the hotel entertainment amusing.

'I'm not exactly a fan of foreign holidays,' he said, 'but even here you get a taste of abroad in the form of the hotel staff. Did you see that hot Russian girl in reception?' I nodded but didn't answer back.

'Several of the staff here are like that. There was a lovely Romanian girl working in the hotel restaurant last year but I haven't seen anything of her as yet this year and even the deputy manager of the hotel has a bang-hot daughter! Last year I saw her in the hotel reception telling her father that she was going to go to a club with a few of her mates. I tell you — the skirt she was wearing must have been modelled off a belt because it was far too short to be considered clothing! I cribbed on where she was going with her mates before I rushed back up to my room and put on my best clothes before heading over to the club in question.'

'Was the club any good?' I asked.

'The bleeding place was a bingo club,' Jack replied. 'She sat there all night with a couple of her mates playing damn bingo! I had a go on one or two of the slot machines before leaving. I did consider sitting at a table nearby and looking at her legs all night to amuse me but the nearest table wasn't anywhere near her.'

Jack decided to leave me a few minutes later because he had seen everything Claptout-by-the-Sea had to offer the last time he was here. He strolled into a pub across the road while I carried on towards the first of the resort's two piers. Rusty Pier was apparently named after the person who commissioned the building of it over one hundred years ago and it was clearly the bigger of the two piers. Stretching out to almost one mile Rusty Pier had a few buildings at the entrance to it, a few other kiosk-like shops littered down the pier itself and a large pavilion building at the end of the pier which, according to posters at the entrance, housed an amusement arcade and a bar with the expected 'End of the Pier' entertainment playing every night. I liked a good stroll along a pier and had enjoyed many a holiday by walking the full length of a pier on a lovely sunny day. Today however the sun was hiding behind a few clouds and there was a slight breeze in evidence but fortunately no rain.

The building at the entrance to Rusty Pier was a family arcade and I spent about half an hour playing on some of the machines for tickets (it had to be tickets because if I wanted to play on the arcades where cash was the prize I would have gone to the local amusements in the city where I lived). After putting ten pounds into a combination of five machines I won a grand total of fifty-seven tickets which I thoughts was okay for a first attempt so I fed them into the obligatory 'ticket crunching' machine that are always in evidence at these places and received a receipt showing how many tickets I had 'crunched'. I then walked out of the arcade and round to a side entrance to the pier which appeared to be the only access point to the pier itself. The walk along the pier reminded me of all of the other piers I had walked along over the years. The boards creaked slightly as I stepped onto them while the slight breeze (which got stronger as I walked nearer to the end of the pier) blew against some of the small kiosks making low noises as the loose glass windows rattled.

The walk along the length of the pier cheered me up and I walked into the pavilion at the end and found myself in another arcade with a cafe and the entrance to the bar clearly signposted. I again spent more cash on the machines and won more tickets (143 this time) and chose to look at the tickets before crunching them in one of the machines. The tickets were primrose yellow in colour and had the words 'Rusty Pier' written in fancy writing on one side and a picture of a cartoon meerkat dressed in combat gear and holding a machine gun on the other side! Rusty Pier certainly knew how to pick its child-friendly mascots!

The bar advertised tonight's entertainment as a blue comedian (no surprise there for a British seaside resort) who had won awards (presumably ones that were awarded for most mother-in-law jokes and most swear words spoken within five minutes). The name of the comedian was Bertie Dastard which had to be a stage name. Surely nobody would have a real name where you could switch around the first letters of both his names to come up with an insult! That aside Bertie seemed to be worth watching but that was merely a guess based solely on his looks so maybe I'd see him tonight. Of course, I wanted to sample a bit of the hotel entertainment first and maybe even take in the live act at the bar recommended by Jack.

I walked back out of the pavilion and past a couple of kids' fairground rides before popping into a kiosk selling fudge with 'Rusty Pier' printed on the box via a postcard that had been glued to the front and also a book detailing the history of the pier. I purchased a box of fudge, an obligatory fridge magnet and also a copy of the book and sat on a wooden bench underneath an awning and read the book. The pier was built in 1895 and commissioned by a bloke called Sir Archibald Rusty who later went on to found a DIY company that produced Rusty Screwdrivers before becoming a victim of a shipwreck in the 1940s when his boat, *The Rusty Ship* sank. Under new ownership, Rusty Pier had a period of non-operation in the early 1970s when it was nothing more than a relic slowly going rusty thus making its name more appropriate! It then reopened in the late 1970s and remained open for a further seven years before the pavilion caught fire! After a rebuild it opened once more in the late 1980s and has remained open ever since.

After reading the book I put it into the bag I had been given and walked back down the pier. I was about to breathe in some of the sea air which always put me in a good mood when it suddenly started to rain. There is always one thing you can guarantee will happen at a British seaside resort and a rainstorm is one such thing. I was only wearing a summer jacket which was hopeless in stopping me from getting wet and I was soaked within seconds as the rain came down harder. My hotel was across the road and a further five minutes' walk down the road. I needed to get across the road but, as is usually the case, everybody seems to want to go for a drive when it's raining. The same is evident where I live and I'm convinced that people look out of the windows of their house and one says to the other, 'Oh look, darling, it's pissing it down. Do you fancy going out for a drive?' Finally, I got across the road and back into the hotel where I quickly rushed up to my room and got dried and changed. It was almost time for the evening meal so I chose clothing that was appropriate for a restaurant even though the restaurant in question was only likely to be nothing better than a posh-looking cafe!

The hotel restaurant was nothing special which was just as I had expected it be. I found my table and discovered that I was paired with an elderly couple who looked like Denis Norden and Dame Edna! Jack sat a few tables away from me and he too was paired with an elderly couple. I smirked as I saw Jack's elderly table guests silently pouring scorn over him as he played games on his mobile while waiting for dinner.

I picked up the menu and flicked through it feeling ever more nauseous with every turn of the page. There was a different page for each day of the week and there seemed to be different things on the menu on each day. I looked down the list of today's choices and selected a salmon fillet drizzled in parsley sauce when the waitress — a lovely looking girl of Eastern European descent walked over to my table and asked for my order as well the orders from Messrs Norden and Everage. The dinner arrived exactly ten minutes later and not only looked slightly cold but also looked like somebody had thrown an old piece of salmon onto a plate and gobbed a mouthful of sauce over it! Because I was starving I duly ate the meal and then washed it down with a cup of tea before ordering dessert. As I drunk the tea I noticed that Jack was staring at the European girl who had served me and also himself a short while later. I guessed that this was the Romanian girl he had spoken of earlier judging by his unwillingness to remove his eyes from the lower half of her body! Jack's table guests were clearly unimpressed with what he was looking at, and muttered something to each other in between quick glances at him. I imagined that they were saying things such as 'such disgrace towards a lady' and 'we never did that in our day. My father would have given me fifty lashes for even looking at a lady's ankle!'

Chapter 3
The First Night

After dinner I left the restaurant amid several suspicious eyes before approaching the reception desk. Bingo tickets were being sold here and a notice taped to the top of the reception desk clearly said, 'Bingo tickets 50p a book — game starts at 7pm in the hotel bar.' I purchased four books and stuffed them in my pocket before walking outside to catch a bit of sea air before the bingo started. A few minutes later Jack exited the hotel.

'Well, that's it,' he said as he lit up a cigarette, 'I'm off to the Punk Establishment then.'

'That's the bar that the band you mentioned is playing at tonight isn't it?' I replied.

'Sure is,' my fellow coach holiday compatriot said between puffs. 'Are you coming?'

'I might pop in,' was my reply. 'What kind of music do they do?'

Jack laughed and almost choked on a mouthful of smoke. 'The bar is called the Punk Establishment so they're not likely to be singing The Birdie Song are they?'

'It would be amusing if they did,' I answered back. Jack had to agree with this. He was fully aware as was I that a punk version of the kids tune Nellie the Elephant had been done in the 1980s so a punk version of The Birdie Song would be highly amusing!

'I would pay good money to see a band do a cover version of that!' Jack said smiling.

What's the name of the band that's playing tonight?' I said finally.

Jack dropped his spent cigarette onto the floor and crushed it underfoot before answering.

'Learning to Piss,' he said, 'they're actually quite good. I saw them last year.'

'Sounds like a bit of an odd name for a band.'

'It would be if you only did pop songs but this is a punk band. The word "piss" is quite a fun word in punk circles. There's another band playing tomorrow night as well that uses the word in their band name as well.'

''What's that band called?' I asked.

'The Six Pissed Dolls!' came Jack's reply.

'That sounds like a female punk band.'

'It is,' smiled Jack, 'six hot babes with cracking legs! They play a mean guitar but their legs are what I go to see!'

'I bet you sit at the front as well don't you? I know a few blokes who would go to see female bands they hate only to look up their skirts! I'm guessing you're one of those people.'

'Of course,' grinned Jack. He then lit up another cigarette and bid me farewell.

I walked back into the hotel and straight into the bar with my bingo tickets in hand. I brought myself a pint of bitter which was viewed with scorn from the gin and tonic drinking elderly guests before sitting down at a vacant table. As I waited for the bingo to start I thought about what I would do with my first night in Claptout-by-the-Sea. I decided to see the live band with Jack but I also wanted to see Bertie Dastard as well. Maybe if the band finished early I'd catch the curiously named comedian but maybe I'd be too late for that.

The hotel bar was certainly spacious and while I sat at the table by myself with my pint there were several other elderly people dotted around the bar drinking gin and tonic or orange juice while waiting eagerly to play bingo. I noticed the elderly couple from the service station who had a habit of reading gardening magazines but not buying them and the man seemed to notice me and sneer at me. Ten minutes later the bingo started. There were four games in the book and the prize money was five pounds for a line and fifteen pounds for a full house. Not bad for the price of the tickets but it wasn't exactly like some of the big bingo casinos around where I lived. The bingo caller was one of the bar staff and, like the restaurant girls, was pretty and not from this country. Despite being a looker and having a sexy accent, she was, however, as annoying as a bingo caller. Almost every number she called she had a rhyming slang term for it and by the end of the first game I had dubbed the hotel bingo as 'Cockney Rhyming Slang Bingo!' Each game seemed to drag on for a lifetime as each individual number commanded about ten seconds of speech but I managed to put up with. I didn't win the first game but I won the second and as I shouted 'house' I noticed the elderly couple from the service station sneer at me once more as if to say, 'You scum! You're too young to be playing bingo — leave it to the more deserving people — us!'

I won a second game as well during the course of the next two games and the elderly couple across the bar gave me another disparaging look. Their facial expressions were priceless and I was determined to play bingo every night of the week and hope to beat them every night just so that I could make their blood boil to extreme temperatures! After the final game had finished I sat back with my second pint and waited for the hotel entertainment to start. Tonight's entertainment was a woman who, judging by the flyer of her pinned to the reception notice board looked like she was in her late forties or early fifties. The flyer claimed that she had a repertoire of over a thousand songs but was quite adept at singing songs by Connie Francis! It was obviously going to be one of those nights that would pan out just as Jack had told me it would.

After another pint of bitter I left the hotel bar. There was only so much one person my age could stand regarding Connie Francis hits and after the fifth consecutive one I had to leave. I had toyed with the idea of waiting around for her to accept requests which I would then request something that wasn't about a century old but the moment never arrived — at least not during the time I sat there! I returned to my hotel room, put on my coat and left the hotel. As I walked along the seafront I pondered who I should see. I had already decided to see the live act but the comedian also interested me somewhat. In the end I made the final decision and walked through the doors of the bar.

The Punk Establishment was a lovely well-kept bar and also quite popular. After I had finally made my way to the bar to order a pint I looked for Jack. If he was here tomorrow when the female punk band would be on all I would have to look for was the stage and I would instantly find him sitting at a table near the front. Tonight however he was sitting a little further back on a small round table that commanded a good view of the stage. I sat opposite him and placed my pint down on the table.

'Learning to Piss are a cracking band,' he explained, 'they do some cracking cover versions of classic punk songs as well as a few of their own compositions.'

'They can't be any worse than the hotel entertainment,' I said.

'Who was on tonight then?' Jack asked.

'Some woman called Vera Donovan who is a specialist at Connie Francis songs,' I replied. Jack almost spat out a mouthful of lager as he heard this.

'She was at the hotel last year,' he revealed. 'She certainly has a large repertoire of songs. All of them are either Connie Francis hits, Connie Francis album tracks, Vera Lynn hits or Vera Lynn album tracks. Like most of these hotel acts she did a request section last year and I asked if she knew anything by Joan Jett and the Blackhearts! She said she didn't but she did know a few songs by Joan Regan and went into one of her hits!'

I then quizzed Jack about the blue comedian known as Bertie Dastard. I was interested to know if he had heard of him and what he was like.

'Yer, I've seen him,' Jack's positive reply was, 'He was performing at Rusty Pier on two nights last year. I couldn't see him on the first night because I was watching the Six Pissed Dolls. I watched Bertie on his second appearance and I have to admit he is good but only as far as seaside comedians go. Don't expect any award-winning performances from him'

'He claims to have won some awards,' I pointed out referring to the poster I had read earlier.

'Yer, most likely a Blue Peter Badge and a Blankety Blank cheque book and pen!' Jack retorted. We then finished our current pints and got another one each before Learning to Piss came on stage.

Learning to Piss were genuinely good. I wasn't exactly a big punk fan (unlike Jack who appeared to idolise the movement) but it's always a sign of a good band when somebody who doesn't much like the music you play finds you entertaining. I would certainly like to see them again if they play anywhere else at some time in the future. At the interval Jack walked outside to light up another cigarette. After he had lit up he handed me a small flyer he had picked up inside.

'This is the band who's playing tomorrow night,' he pointed out.

'They look quite nice,' I commented as I looked at the picture on the flyer of six attractive young women wearing punk style miniskirts and short dresses while holding their respective instruments.

'They certainly are,' smiled Jack, 'as I've already said you can't miss a performance from them. The sight of their legs is worth the entrance price alone!'

'Do you only ever talk about women and certain parts of their anatomy?' I said.

'Yep,' he grinned, 'why? Don't you?'

'Not really,' I replied, 'I see women for what they are.'

'So do I,' said Jack, 'I see them as hotties with cracking legs!'

After the cigarette break we returned to see the second half of the bands set which was just as good as the first half. The gig didn't finish until almost midnight and after we had finished our respective drinks we walked back to the hotel. As we did so I was wondering if the main doors of the hotel were locked up for the night. The last coach holiday I went on dropped us off at a hotel where they locked up at 11 pm and I had to ask the security guard to let me back in. I remember the guard giving me a funny look as if to say 'bleeding lager lout! Why don't you get in bed by ten o'clock like everybody else in the hotel!' I asked Jack if he knew.

'The hotel can't afford a security guard,' he said to my relief. 'They do lock up the main door but only when the receptionist finishes at two in the morning. It then remains locked until 7 am when the morning staff arrive.'

'How do you know this?' I asked.

'I came into the hotel at half past one on one of the nights,' he admitted. 'I then tried to chat up the receptionist but she said she was leaving at two o'clock and locking up the hotel. As for me knowing what time they unlock the main door, I got up early on another morning to try and chat up another receptionist but it turned out she was already being boned by one of the male restaurant staff!'

We walked into the hotel reception and past the entrance to the bar which was now eerily quiet. The singer had long since finished and her audience had gone up to bed. Jack's room was on the floor below mine so we parted company on his floor and I walked up to my room. I entered my room, shut the door behind me and turned on the light. Only two of the five available lights worked but it was just enough to find out where my bed was. I collapsed onto it and, like earlier on, the legs of the bed collapsed in mock sympathy! I seriously needed to report this problem to reception which I promised myself I would do first thing in the morning. I again hastily repaired the legs and got changed into my bedclothes before climbing into bed. The bed itself wasn't exactly the most comfortable but it would suit me for the following week. Tomorrow would be a full day of leisure around Claptout-by-the-Sea where I would explore more of the resort and buy more fridge magnets and a few sticks of rock. I would also walk down to the resort's second pier which was in the 'posh' district where all of the main attractions were. For now, however, it was the end of day one and I was tired.

Chapter 4
The Next Day

I woke up early the following morning to discover that my bed had collapsed again overnight. I looked at the time on my mobile phone that I had left on the bedside cabinet and sighed. It was half past six in the morning. HALF PAST SIX! I DIDN'T GO ON HOLIDAY TO WAKE UP AT AROUND THE SAME TIME I GET UP FOR WORK FIVE DAYS A WEEK! I couldn't get back to sleep and besides, a shaft of sunlight came in through a small hole in one of the curtains. I yawned, had a shower and got dressed before undrawing the curtains to look outside. It was a lovely day so maybe I could take an early morning stroll before breakfast at eight thirty.

I left my hotel room and found that I wasn't the only one up. There were a select few hotel guests wandering around admiring the hotel wallpaper and one or two pictures hung up on the walls while a few others were looking into glass cabinets that displayed pens and notebooks for sale with the hotel name printed on them. I walked past the reception and took a quick glance at the attractive female behind the desk. I wonder if she was the one who Jack had tried to chat up last year? I left the hotel and found Jack already outside smoking a cigarette.

'Hi, Jack,' I said smiling as I looked up at the blue sky. 'Couldn't you sleep either?'

'It's damn near difficult to sleep when half of the guests

at the hotel like to get up and potter around at about five in the morning! I reckon they go sleep throughout the day in their hotel rooms just so that they can get up at silly o'clock every morning!'

Jack flicked the butt of his cigarette onto the road outside the hotel and turned to me.

'Have you ever been on a coach holiday like this before?' he asked.

'I went on one last year but not with this coach company. Why?'

'Because normally the oldies on these trips form a long queue outside of the restaurant every morning about an hour before their scheduled breakfast time. Last year I was here I tried to go out for a fag but a queue of oldies blocked the door like the Berlin Wall! It'll be the same again this year so just be prepared for it.'

'How can you prepare for something like that?' I said.

'I suppose you could see if one of the gift shops sells pairs of stilts so that you can just walk over the top of the queue. Failing that I suggest you look for a pair of 1970s Noddy Holder boots or a pogo stick!'

Jack was right. At exactly 7.45 a queue outside of the restaurant had formed and it was nigh on impossible to reach the exit of the hotel if you had just left your room. After Jack had gone back into the hotel following his cigarette break I had taken the quick stroll I had promised myself. There was a little breeze in the air but nothing too windy. I had crossed over the road and walked along the beach which was littered with seaweed and dog excrement before returning to the hotel. I was standing near the hotel exit while on the other side of the human wall was Jack. Presumably he wanted another cigarette but the queue of oldies prevented him from doing so. Suddenly I heard Jack shout 'stink bomb!' and then a slight tap on the floor as something left his hand. Moments later the human wall dispersed in all directions with each individual holding their noses as Jack walked towards the exit.

'What did you do?' I asked him.

'I said to be prepared for such an occasion,' he replied, 'and I was. I picked up a stink bomb from a joke shop on the back streets yesterday and let it off right in the centre of that queue of oldies!'

'That certainly worked,' I said chuckling.

'It certainly did,' smiled the prankster as he looked back and noticed the oldies catching their breath as they sat down on dining chairs, stairs and also standing against various walls breathing heavily!

I leaned against a wall outside the hotel while Jack stood facing me smoking another cigarette. As he puffed away I looked over his shoulder and noticed a laundry van just about to drive off. As the driver put his (or her) foot on the pedal the nearside back door of the van flew open and deposited a bag of soiled towels onto the road. I stared aghast as the driver just drove off clearly not noticing that he (or she) had dropped one of their bags. Quite why the driver never noticed through their wing mirror that one of the back doors were open is anyone's guess but Jack looked at me incredulously as I stared over his shoulder. He turned around just as the van turned a corner and disappeared from view and he looked at the errant bag of laundry which had now come open and spilled some of its contents out onto the road before turning back to face me to ask what had just happened. I explained the event I had just witnessed and he laughed!

Moments later the receptionist came outside — another victim of Jack's stink bomb. She coughed as she leaned against the wall while Jack stood there admiring her from the waist down.

'Hello babe,' smiled Jack, 'what's wrong?'

'What's wrong?' coughed the young girl, 'you — that's what's wrong! How could you do something like that? I could have fainted!'

'That wouldn't be a problem,' replied the prankster, 'I'd only be too happy to give you mouth-to-mouth!'

'I bet you would as well you dirty pervert!' spat the receptionist. She then took a lungful of air and walked back inside. Both me and Jack laughed even though I at least knew it was immoral.

I walked into the hotel restaurant at exactly the correct time as stated on the piece of card that came with my room key. Everage and Norden were already sitting at the table and so were the elderly couple who sat with Jack. Jack had yet to arrive because he felt that having another cigarette was imminently more important than a sub-standard breakfast! Judging by how much Everage and Norden had eaten of their breakfast it was obvious that they had sat down at the table some time earlier than the stated time. I waited for one of the restaurant staff to approach the table and when one did, I ordered a coffee and a traditional fried breakfast. While I waited I looked at the woman who looked like Dame Edna Everage and was convinced that the person was actually a man dressed as a woman! Of course, I was likely to be wrong but it was something that would no doubt occupy my mind for the duration of today's breakfast.

My traditional breakfast arrived along with the coffee and

a rack of toast and as I started on the breakfast the staff member who had brought it me explained that the Chef's Special for tonight's dinner was beef curry. This seemed to be something that all hotels who accepted coach holiday guests did. As well as the regular slop that was on offer on the menu there was also a Chef's Special that would only be made if a guest asked for it at breakfast time. I declined the Chef's Special but I guessed that Jack would accept it just so that he could drop a few more stink bombs at dinner and claim that the curry was already making its way through his system!

I finished my breakfast and also two rounds of toast while Everage and Norden were making their way through their first round of toast each. They were clearly slow eaters and that convinced me more that they had arrived in the hotel restaurant far earlier than I had first thought otherwise they would not have been able to have eaten as much of their breakfast as they had before my arrival. After the toast, I finished my coffee and got up to leave just as Jack entered the restaurant and sat down. As he did so I craned my neck around to see what his elderly table guests thought of his late arrival. They appeared to look at him with disgust and then look at the time on their wrist watches each before comparing times and tutting! Jack was oblivious to their disgust which got even more intense as he pulled out his mobile phone and began to play a game on it!

After a brief return to my hotel room, I left the hotel and went for a walk along the seafront. As I stood on the beach I observed a man taking his dog for a walk. The dog then relieved itself and the man picked up the waste in a small plastic bag. 'At least some people have got some decency,' I said to myself but then I watched as the dog owner pulled a catapult out of his jacket pocket and loaded the bagged waste into it. He then pulled it back, aimed far out to sea and released it! As the waste landed with a visible but not audible plop out to sea I leaned back against a concrete sea wall that separated the coastal road from the beach.

After a quick round on the amusements on Rusty Pier I walked a little further up the road and found a waxworks museum. Normally these places had wax models that were a work of art but I had heard that the one at Claptout-by-the-Sea was one of the worst in the country. Intrigued, I stepped inside and paid the admission fee of seven pounds which sounded quite cheap and reasonable but it was most likely the going rate for a seemingly poor quality exhibit. Inside were a series of rooms where various wax dummies of famous people stood… or at least they were supposed to be of famous people! One dummy wore a smart grey/blue suit with white shirt and blue tie and was holding a stack of question cards. I looked hard at the face but couldn't recognise the person at all. I then looked at the sign standing beside the dummy which identified him and it claimed he was the host of a famous quiz show I watched on a regular basis back home. I looked at the face again and then at the identification sign and then at the face again but I couldn't seem to connect the two together. It was like passing a Japanese martial arts movie star off as Father Christmas!

More followed and I had to look at the identification card to guess who the person was. Sports stars, movie stars, TV stars, models — they were all there and all of them I knew from the identification card only. The models looked nothing like who they were supposed to be. One such model claimed to be of a young football star who was currently nineteen years of age but the waxwork model of him made him look like a pensioner with back trouble! A blonde-haired male footballer looked like a female supermodel and a female supermodel looked like a male dictator of a foreign land! It was all too much for me to take! After giving up trying to identify a model of somebody holding a microphone and having a guitar slung around himself I gave up! At the end of the exhibit I walked into the shop, brought a couple of fridge magnets with the museums name on it as well as a pen, pencil and eraser before walking out.

Next door to the house of horrors (as I liked to call it) was an aquarium. A staple of British holiday resorts this was a giant marine museum of sorts that housed tropical fish including sharks in large tanks. I've been to a few in my time and they have never ceased to amaze me. Some have been good but others have been laughably lame! Claptout-by-the-Sea's aquarium was called 'Claptout Cove' and boasted that it contained almost a thousand different marine wildlife. After paying the ten pounds to gain entrance I soon discovered that it was run by the same company as the wax museum which set alarm bells ringing in my head. As I walked around Claptout Cove I admired some of the large tanks where various forms of tropical and Atlantic fish dwelled but other features such as a couple of terrapins with limps, a shark that wanted to go sleep on top of a walkthrough glass tunnel all the time and a tank with a few dead fish floating on top of the water were not so entertaining. A mother and child were walking around in front of me and the kid noticed a dead fish floating on the surface of the water in its respective tank.

'Why is that fish floating on the water?' asked the inquisitive child to her mother.

'He's just having a sleep,' came the logical reply, 'he's had a very hard day!'

The child seemed satisfied with that answer and they continued walking. I finished my little jaunt through Claptout Cove by studying a couple of empty fish tanks before walking into the gift shop at the end where I purchased more fridge magnets, pens and pencils. I then headed out to see what else I could find.

I still had a few more hours to kill before I had to return to the hotel for dinner with Everage and Norden. I stumbled upon a side street just a few metres away from the aquarium and decided to walk down it. This was obviously the shopping area of the resort and it featured a large selection of high street shops that had nothing to do with my definition of a holiday resort but crucially a few gift shops and amusement arcades. I spent a few quid in the first arcade I found which was called 'The Penny Drops' before heading into one next door called 'Silver Fruits'. After this arcade there were a row of ten high street shops where I found a few of the hotel residents browsing around inside. This wasn't surprising because on previous coach holidays the elderly residents seemed to only go to a seaside resort to buy things that they can just as easily purchase in their own town centre nearer to their home. I watched as I noticed the sneering elderly couple from last night's bingo walk out of a supermarket with what appeared to be their weekly grocery shopping! I pulled my mobile phone out of my pocket just to check the day and then watched as Mr and Mrs Sneer walked back to the hotel with two bags of shopping each. We still had another five days here at Claptout-by-the-Sea and this couple were doing their grocery shopping in readiness for their first day back in their own house! There was no fridge or freezer in the hotel rooms so I wondered where they were going to keep the fresh and frozen produce they had just brought!

Just as I was about to walk past the supermarket I noticed Jack inside. There was no way he was going to do the same as Mr and Mrs Sneer and I was right. He had brought a couple of bottles of cheap German lager and instead of just paying for them and leaving he chose to chat up one of the checkout operatives. I couldn't hear what he was saying but I guessed the conversation went something like this:

'Hey babe, are you single?'

'Get lost creep!'

'Don't be like that gorgeous, I like a girl in uniform so we would get on like a house on fire!'

'I wish you were trapped in a house on fire!'

Maybe I have an overactive imagination but I was pretty certain the conversation went along those lines!

After watching Mr and Mrs Sneer walk off into the distance and back to the hotel I carried onwards down this side street whereupon I found another arcade called 'Golden Showers'. Another ten pounds of my holiday money was spent here before I left. It was at this point that I noticed Jack walking out of a joke shop a few doors down from the arcade (presumably the same joke shop he had brought the stink bombs from yesterday). He noticed me and walked over to me to show me what he had brought. Plastic dog excrement and a bag of small stink bombs that you crushed in your hand to give off the smell seemed to be his only two purchases and he explained that they would both come in use in the hotel restaurant tonight.

'Let me guess,' I said to the prankster, 'you've ordered the chef's special curry and you're going to pretend that it's going right through you while you eat it and let off a stink bomb?'

Jack grinned. 'You know me too well!' He replied.

Jack then walked into a nearby pub despite already purchasing two bottles of lager (he seemed to spend more time in pubs here than seeing the sights) while I walked back onto the seafront to explore the rest of the resort.

Next up was a crazy golf course and also a ferris wheel. I loved playing a game of crazy golf and always endeavoured to play at least once at every holiday resort I visited. A couple of years ago I went to a holiday resort where there were no less than four crazy golf courses within a twenty-minute walk along the seafront and I went on a crazy golf bender by playing on all four of them consecutively! The competitive nature inside me got out of control on one of the courses where a couple and their young son were on the hole ahead of me and I pushed myself to play better than the kid! It was on hole nine on this course where the young child only managed one under par but when I set foot on the course I aimed for a hole-in-one. To my surprise I got it but before moving onto the next hole I celebrated by doing a little dance (which left some of the other players scratching their heads) and also pointing at the child and boasting, 'I'm better than you,' about three times over!

The crazy golf course at Claptout-by-the-Sea had a pirate theme which, I believe, is a standard theme for many crazy golf courses at holiday resorts because two of the four courses I went on at the other holiday resort were also pirate themed. I paid for my ball and club and then started to play, assuming a normal golfer's stance (I have to point out here that I'm not a professional golfer and my 'golfer's stance' isn't the same kind of stance Tiger Woods would assume but rather one that Bugs Bunny would assume in a cartoon!). Hole one was fairly easy and I managed one-under par but the next three holes were better best forgotten. Hole two saw me hit the ball too hard, bounce off a wooden fence (which looked like the remains of a shipwreck) and then back into the hole one course! Hole three saw the ball land in a small river of water and hole four saw me picking the ball back up from out of the hole one course again! There were fifteen holes in all and I succeeded in getting under par in eight of them. It wasn't that big a loss but I have done better. What did annoy me, however, was that a damn little kid mocked me on hole twelve because he got a hole-in-one and I dropped my ball in the water! I mean, you'd never see me mocking a kid if I did better than him!

After leaving the crazy golf course by means of a pirate-themed exit that looked like a hole in the side of a wrecked ship I ventured towards the Ferris wheel. I have to point out another flaw with myself here. I'm afraid of heights and Ferris wheels do not sit well with me. For some reason though I always want to go on a Ferris wheel. Maybe it's the thought of getting to the very top and getting an excellent view of the entire holiday resort that persuades me to go on them. I paid to go on the Ferris wheel and sat down in one of the buckets (I don't know what they're actually called but I like to call them buckets due to them seemingly swinging back and forth when the wheel is in motion as if they are real buckets being held by somebody walking to a well or something else where the bucket is needed). The Ferris wheel started up and it slowly climbed to the top as I clung onto the sides with fright! In the bucket below me there was the same kid who had mocked me on the crazy golf course who was jumping up and down excitedly in his seat in between his parents. 'Please stop jumping around!' I said to myself as I clung onto the sides tighter but the kid didn't. My bucket reached the very top… and then stopped. 'Shit!' I thought, 'the thing has broken down!' The kid below me was still jumping up and down and I closed my eyes and tried to think of other things. My mind however was playing tricks on me and all I could think of was an image of the kid jumping up and down until the tethers holding the buckets to the Ferris wheel snapped! I opened my eyes and focused on the view instead but all I could see were grotty rooftops and dogs using the beach as a toilet. Eventually, the Ferris wheel started moving again and it completed ten full rotations before it stopped to let me off. I stumbled off the ride as if drunk and grabbed onto some nearby railings while I caught my breath before finding a bench to sit down on.

It took me ten minutes to recover and when I stood back up I looked at the Ferris wheel and said to myself 'never again' even though I would no doubt be persuaded to go on another one at another holiday resort next year! I walked onwards passing a water fountain that wasn't fully working and a few small seafront gardens before I reached Claptout-by-the-Sea's second pier. Claptout Pier was significantly longer than Rusty Pier and was a more family friendly one. The arcades were more dedicated to kids' rides and the shops and kiosks sold mostly stuffed toys and colouring books. I walked along the full length of the pier and looked at the beach below me as adults wrote swear words in the sand with sticks while kids kicked beach balls around occasionally hitting a dog having a toilet break! I brought some Claptout-by-the-Sea fudge as well as a few sticks of rock and more fridge magnets with the pier name on them before walking into the pavilion which was nothing more than a large arcade with a small fast food kiosk built against one wall as an afterthought. I treated myself to a hot dog before playing on several of the ticket-producing fruit machines. I went on one of the machines and only won ten tickets despite stuffing a little over ten pounds into the machine before moving onto the next machine. The crazy golf/Ferris wheel kid then turned up and had a go on the machine I had just vacated and I seethed with anger as his twenty pence won him over 500 tickets!

I had better luck on some of the other machines however and ended my gambling stint with a total of 207 tickets. I looked at the tickets before crunching them in the obligatory ticket crunching machine and was certain that Claptout Pier' s mascot was the brother of Rusty Pier's mascot. A cartoon meerkat dressed as a ninja and wielding a collection of daggers and throwing stars surely couldn't have been child-friendly but Claptout Pier seemed to have no problem.

After leaving the arcade I cautiously ventured outside making sure that it wasn't raining or was going to rain. The sun was out but there was a little wind. This was to be expected if you are standing at the very end of a pier so this didn't alarm me. Just like Rusty Pier there was another small gift shop midway across the boardwalk which sold 'A History of…' guide book. I brought a copy of the book and then flicked through it before stumbling on another hot dog stand. I'm a glutton for hot dogs whenever I go on holiday and I have been known to eat five in a row before! I brought a hot dog and started eating it before leaning over the side of the pier to look down on the beach. Suddenly, the hot dog sausage slipped out from the bun and down onto the beach hitting a yob on the top of the head just as he was about to write an expletive in the sand! I stepped back so that he wouldn't notice me and threw the empty bun in a rubbish bin.

I walked along the full length of the pier and then out onto the promenade before heading across the road and then onwards towards my hotel. I must have been only about two minutes away from the hotel when the rain came down suddenly. Again, I was soaked but fortunately not as much this time as I was last time. As soon as I walked into my room I was relieved to find that the room service had been and had tidied up my room as well as replenishing the stock of tea, coffee and milk. After drying myself off I changed into clothing that was to become the ones I would wear to the restaurant a little later, and made a cup of tea before sitting by the window and watching the rain come down.

The bad weather had stopped by the time lunch was served in the restaurant. I entered the hotel restaurant about fifteen minutes after my scheduled time to avoid what I liked to call 'the Pensioners Rush' and sat down at my table where Norden and Everage had already finished their starters and were waiting for the main course. Jack still wasn't present and his table guests appeared to be keeping a tab on how late he was. The elderly couple appeared to be comparing wrist watches and tutting as if they had some kind of moral obligation to look after him! Little did they know what Jack had in store for them!

I ordered a plate of small hard black disks covered in vomit (or, as the menu called it 'black pudding in creamy black peppercorn sauce') while Norden and Everage tucked into their main course. Jack then made an appearance and Mr and Mrs Stopwatch compared their watches once more and tutted again as he sat down. I then tucked into my main course of wet brown slices of meat with grass cuttings (or, as the menu called it 'lamb with mint sauce'). Jack started to tuck into his chef's special of beef curry and as he did so he palmed one of his mini stink bombs. I watched with a slight smirk on my face as he let off the first one and accompanied it with the words 'Damn it. Curry always goes through me like diarrhoea!' Unsurprisingly, Mr and Mrs Stopwatch stopped eating their meal as did one or two other elderly couples sitting at nearby tables! The faces of Mr and Mrs Stopwatch were priceless as they drew in deep breaths before looking at Jack with complete disgust! Both me and Jack ordered cheese and biscuits for desert while Mr and Mrs Stopwatch left their table still retching slightly from the smell. Shortly afterwards I left and stood outside the hotel to catch a bit more of the sea air.

A few minutes later Jack joined me outside and lit up a cigarette.

'Did you like that?' he asked me with a smirk.

'Of course,' I said, 'did you know that they were keeping tabs on you and checking which time you turned up?'

'I know,' replied Jack, 'their room is a few doors down from mine and I watched them leave for the restaurant about twenty minutes before their allotted time. I suppose it takes them about ten minutes to get down the stairs or to step into the elevator though.'

'I thought you were going to use the fake dog mess in the restaurant this evening?' I then asked him.

'I was going to,' came the reply, 'I was thinking of putting it on one of their empty plates but then I thought better of it.'

'That doesn't sound like you,' I said curiously.

'Don't get me wrong,' explained the prankster, 'I'm still going to use it — I'm going to put it outside their hotel room door a little later so that they wake up the following morning and see it!'

As Jack stubbed out his cigarette on an ornate plaster feature bordering the front door of the hotel he asked me if I was going to see tonight's gig at The Punk Establishment.

'I certainly am,' I smiled, 'but I'll be playing a game of Cockney Rhyming Slang Bingo first in the hotel bar and checking out the crap that passes for entertainment first though.'

'Tonight's rubbish is a bloke who looks like Des O'Connor,' said Jack.

'You mean Des O'Connor in his prime?' I asked.

'No,' explained Jack, 'Des O'Connor how he looks today! According to the flyer pinned up on the notice board in reception he looks like he needs a Zimmer frame just to get to the stage!'

Chapter 5
Watching The Dolls

It struck me suddenly that I was a curious breed when on holiday. Most people enjoyed their nights by doing one thing they loved and never straying into other interests but I was different. I was juggling my nights between playing bingo and watching punk bands — both of which go together about as well as chocolate and mashed potatoes! After purchasing the bingo tickets from reception I walked into the hotel bar and ordered a drink before choosing a seat directly opposite Mr and Mrs Sneer. The elderly couple looked at me and gave me a funny look as I sat down hinting that they were annoyed that I had even bothered to turn up to play bingo! Unknown to them however I was a regular at my local bingo casino back home and had been for quite some time. Most Friday nights I could be found in my local Jackpot Casino playing bingo for two hundred quid a house — something that the Sneer duo probably thought was silly! In fact, when I first arrived here in Claptout-by-the-Sea, the coach travelled past a Jackpot Casino place which meant that I could use my membership card to get inside sometime and have a few games and maybe even win a bit of holiday money.

As I scanned the rest of the bar, I noticed Mr and Mrs Stopwatch sitting a few seats down from me comparing watches again presumably annoyed that the bingo wasn't starting precisely on time. Eventually though the bingo did start and I got close to winning the first game before winning the second. The look on the faces of Mr and Mrs Sneer was incredible as they shot me an evil glance each before taking a sip of their bitter lemon and tonic water in unison! Unfortunately for me this was the only game of bingo I won tonight and, after it was finished I sat around for twenty minutes before the Des O'Connor lookalike turned up. He was every bit as Jack had described him as and his music appeared to be just as old as himself! After singing a couple of songs by Nat 'King' Cole I finished my drink and walked back to my hotel room to change into something more befitting my next choice of drinking establishment.

The Punk Establishment was a little more crowded than it had been the previous night. I found Jack sitting alone at a small table near the stage and, after picking myself up a pint of bitter from the bar I joined him.

'I had to get a table near the stage,' explained Jack as he took a sip of his drink. 'The Six Pissed Dolls are amazing so you've got to get as close to them as possible.'

'Let me guess,' I commented, 'they're amazing from the waist down?'

'Of course,' smirked Jack, 'and I'd be mightily disappointed if they didn't wear their trademark miniskirts so that I could see right up their...'

Jack didn't need to finish the sentence before a compére walked on stage and announced the nigh'ts live act.

'Tonight, we have the lovely Six Pissed Dolls,' he announced, 'an act who is well known in this part of the country for their excellent performances...'

'...and their excellent legs,' whispered Jack.

'...and their equally fantastic stage persona.' The compére

finished. He then walked off the stage as six young females wearing sexy punk outfits walked on.

Jack wasn't wrong about a certain part of their anatomy but their singing was also good and I found myself enjoying a genre of music that prior to this holiday I hadn't even considered listening to in any kind of depth. After they had performed their first song which was one of their own compositions called 'Punk All Night' the lead singer introduced the band.

'Hello everybody,' shouted the lead singer who sounded less pissed than her band name implied. 'My name is Emily Jones and I'm the lead singer of the Six Pissed Dolls.' She then held out a hand to the guitarist on her left to introduce her. 'This here is Jenny Statham — the amazing lead guitarist in the band,' (Jenny played a few notes on her guitar after being introduced) 'and here on my right is rhythm guitarist Liz Parsons,' (again, a few notes from the recently introduced musician) 'and standing next to her is bass guitarist Tracey Turner,' (a couple of bass riffs echoed through the room). 'At the back of the stage is drummer Katie Moore,' (a quick drum solo was dutifully pounded out) 'and finally we have keyboardist Wendy Reid,' (a tinkling of the keys ensued). After the band had been formally introduced they went straight into their next song which was an excellent punk cover version of the ballad, 'My Heart Will Go On.'

Another seven songs were performed before the band took a break just like Learning to Piss did the previous night. Jack went outside for a cigarette and I followed him with a pint of bitter in my hand.

'So what did you think of them?' the punk fanatic quizzed.

'They were really good,' I replied, 'some of their songs

were amazing.'

'No, I don't mean their music,' he said, 'I'm talking about their bodies!'

'How did I guess that this conversation would end up going this way?'

'Perhaps you know me too well,' he smiled, 'so what did you think of their bodies then?'

'They were quite nice,' I said trying to sound less modest than I really was.

'Really nice!' Jack echoed, 'they were incredible! I spent much of the night looking up Jenny's skirt! Did you know she's wearing white knickers tonight?'

'I do now,' I replied as I took a sip of my beer. 'Did you notice any other attributes relating to female undergarments that you might think I should be interested in or were the guitarists knickers your sole focus of attention?'

'No need to be sarcastic,' said Jack as he flicked his cigarette end over a wall of the beer garden. Suddenly, I heard somebody shout, 'Oi, bastard!' over the wall. Jack looked around and noticed that his cigarette end had hit a passer-by in the face and that person was now showing his disgust. Jack apologised before lighting up another cigarette.

I got myself another beer and then we went in to see the second half of the Six Pissed Dolls act. Some of the songs that the group performed were the standard covers of well-known punk songs (some of which I didn't recognise but Jack pointed out who sung the original versions) but other songs were ones they had written themselves including one that I was convinced was titled 'Tickled Punk' (it probably was as that was the only phrase I could understand in the whole song!). Jack had switched seats and was now looking up Tracey's skirt whilst pretending to enjoy the music and nothing else. At one point I was sure that the bass guitarist had noticed where Jack's eyes were pointing and had moved a little way out of his eye line as a result. The second half of the gig lasted a little under fifty minutes — just as the first half had done and during the entire gig me and Jack must have drunk several pints of alcohol each. We staggered out of the venue close to midnight and proceeded back to the hotel. The night was cool and calm and I expected it to rain as it normally did but thankfully it didn't. Again, the main door was locked and we had to be let in by the receptionist who I thought kept the door open until she left at 2am. Jack assumed that it was because she thought that nobody else was going to come into the hotel at midnight so she decided to lock up. I went straight up to my hotel room but Jack stayed down in the reception, trying to chat up the girl there without any degree of success.

Back in my room I sat in a chair drinking a cup of tea and thought about the night. The band were actually quite good and I would go as far as to say that they were better than several professional groups that were currently in the charts. Jack was also right about their looks and they certainly turned a few heads — including mine. I began to wonder when they would be playing next and if it would be during the course of my holiday. I then drank my tea and promptly fell asleep in the chair!

Chapter 6
A Whole Lot of Claptrap

I woke up the following morning early as expected. The previous night had taken its toll on me and I had a slight hangover as a result. It was seven o'clock in the morning and there was already much shuffling around outside my door. The other hotel guests that I had to share the coach with today en route to Claptrap were already up and about making sure that everybody else was awake by carefully choosing the floorboards along the landing which creaked the most and walking only on those ones!

I got up, showered and shaved before enjoying a cup of coffee in my room as I looked out of my hotel room window. It was a nice clear day — the kind of one that put me in a good mood but the sight of overflowing dustbins sitting on a backyard wasn't something which lifted my spirits. I therefore decided to leave the hotel and have a quick walk around before breakfast. I walked along the main road running along the seafront for almost half an hour before walking back along the beach which was still a little soggy from the high tide of the previous night. When I returned to the hotel I found Jack standing outside having his obligatory cigarette. As soon as he saw me he walked over to me and asked if I had liked last night's gig at The Punk Establishment. I gave him a positive answer which delighted him and then I asked if there was anything good on there tonight.

'No there isn't,' was his reply, 'but I'm still going in there for a drink anyway. That comedian Bertie Dastard is on tonight on Rusty Pier though if you want to see him.'

'I might just do that,' I replied, 'are you going to see him as well?'

'Nah!' Jack said. 'I've seen him before. He's okay but he's not brilliant. You might like him though so don't let me stop you seeing him.'

With that Jack stubbed out his cigarette on the side of the hotel and walked back inside.

The obligatory queue for the restaurant was in evidence again and we both had to fight our way to our respective hotel rooms which we eventually managed and then we went down to the restaurant a few minutes past our scheduled time. I sat at my table just as Norden and Everage was finishing their breakfast and Jack sat at his just as Mr and Mrs Stopwatch stopped comparing times on their watches. Both me and Jack ate a full English breakfast each and then was asked if we would like the Chef's Special for dinner tonight. The special was apparently Chilli Con Carne which I liked so I ordered it hoping that it would be better than any of the slop that was on the main menu.

About an hour after breakfast all of us were standing outside the hotel waiting for our coach to arrive to take us on the day trip to Claptrap. While we waited I pondered about the route the driver was going to take. It was only a twenty-minute drive to Claptrap from Claptout-by-the-Sea but the driver would no doubt make it last a full hour! He had already admitted that he was going to drive through a few picturesque villages en route which seemed to be a bad choice because the only villages in this area which could be labelled as 'picturesque' were in the opposite direction. I assumed he was going to leave Claptout-by-the-Sea going north to reach these villages before travelling back south skirting around the outside of Claptout-by-the-Sea and reaching Claptrap that way!

Eventually the coach arrived and we all got on board. As soon as we were settled and the driver had done a head count he set off and, as predicted, he travelled north. As we exited Claptout-by-the-Sea I looked around the coach to find something — anything — to amuse me. I noticed one of the coach's emergency exit devices — the trusty hammer, and read the instructions that came with it. On each of the windows on the coach a message read 'to break glass use hammer' and located on the ceiling of the coach was a small sealed box with the hammer inside it with a glass lid to protect it. On the glass lid a message read 'to retrieve hammer break glass' which got me thinking. If you needed the hammer to break one of the windows what did you need to break the glass that was covering the hammer? If you found something you could use to break the glass lid protecting the hammer what was stopping the person from using the same item to save time and break the window with the same item? Sometimes safety measures just weren't thought out properly!

Just as I was about to ponder something else the driver switched on his microphone and caught everybody's attention by belching! After this he began a long-winded talk about the villages we were just about to go through. 'We will soon be arriving in the picturesque village of Drizzle where it nearly always rains but on a fine day you can stand and admire the rows and rows of thatched houses and old farms. We will then travel on towards Grass-on-the-Hill which is a lovely village featuring a few thatched houses and lots of scenic hillsides and lakes. After this we will travel towards Bucket and then Puddle where we will find more thatched houses to admire before we arrive in Claptrap.' The driver then belched once more as a means of signing off.

After about ten minutes we arrived in the village of Drizzle where, true to form, it was wet! While all of the elderly passengers were looking out of the windows admiring all of the thatched houses and waterlogged fields and commenting on how beautiful it all looked, I slumped down in my seat and tried to get a bit of sleep. Moments later we drove through Grass-on-the-Hill and what should have been a quick five-minute jaunt through the village turned out to be a fifteen-minute problem drive as the driver took us down a tight one-way street only to discover that he couldn't get all the way down the road due to parked cars on both sides of the road! I waited on the coach while the driver got off and knocked on several doors down the road asking if they could move their cars! A few car owners refused to do so and even criticized the driver for taking such a silly route while others obliged and moved their cars. While all of this was going on several of the elderly passengers also departed the bus to stand on the pavement and look at many of the thatched houses. Eventually we got going but not before all of the elderly passengers had very slowly boarded the coach once more.

More drama ensued in Bucket when the driver took us down another tight one way street and promptly hit a parked car causing the car owner to run out of his house waving his fists and shouting at the driver! They then exchanged insurance details and as the driver got back on the coach I heard the disgruntled car owner say, 'Bleeding fat bastard driver. Why doesn't he drive down the fucking motorway like everybody else with a brain!' I then overheard the car owner's neighbour (who was standing next to him) say in reply, 'He didn't use the motorway because the fat bastard was most likely too busy eating a double cheeseburger and he missed the turn-off!' Finally we set back off and headed towards Puddle which we travelled through unscathed despite driving down yet another tight one-way street and only just navigating past parked cars.

Finally, after over an hour we were in Claptrap. The place hadn't changed much in the almost twenty years since I came here on a school trip. The coach parked in a small coach park alongside three other holiday tour buses from rival companies such as Pratt's (a coach company founded by some bloke called Pratt who most likely only attracted people who could be described as prats), Crap Coaches (again, a company founded by somebody called Crap) and Golden Stream Travel. As most of the elderly passengers slowly walked towards the main door of the coach to depart me and Jack went out of the now open side door and had already started walking while most of the coach were still trying to get off.

We had six hours to kill in Claptrap according to the coach driver and Jack suggested we spend some of that in a local pub! I said that I might do that for about an hour near the end of the day trip but not straight away. The first thing on my list of things to do was to find a gift shop so that I could purchase a few fridge magnets and before long I found just such a place. The gift shop had a nice selection of stuff and I ended up buying not just fridge magnets but also a guide book, a mug and a couple of bookmarks! Me and Jack then progressed further and my esteemed travel companion seemed to be delighted when he set eyes on a cobbler's shop. I was curious as to why he found such a place so fascinating so I asked him.

'You see that sign outside the shop,' he said pointing to a sign which read 'watch batteries fitted here', 'well, I'm going to go inside and ask the shop owner if I can watch a battery being fitted! After all, it says you can do such a thing on that sign!' I facepalmed myself as I got the gist of the prank just as Jack walked inside. I stayed outside the shop but could hear what he was saying to the shopkeeper. True to his word Jack asked the request and as expected the shopkeeper was bamboozled by it before telling the prankster to leave. Jack did so with a smirk on his face and we continued onwards.

It wasn't long before we found a pub in Claptrap which Jack quickly raced towards. I had already decided not to spend the entire day trip in the pub so I bid him farewell for the moment as I continued to explore this sleepy village. Over the course of the next hour I visited several shops all lined up down a small cobbled street. In each shop I purchased a couple of things each ranging from locally cooked shortbread to postcards (a man can never have enough postcards to prove he has visited the place) and even a lovely porcelain plate with the name Claptrap written on it along with several pictures depicting the various landmarks of the village. At the end of this high street I found Claptrap Cathedral which was more of a tourist attraction than a place of worship these days and, eager to look inside I ventured forth.

The entrance fee was a quite reasonable five pounds so I paid up and walked around inside where many other tourists were also to be found. I've always been fascinated by old buildings such as castles and churches and Claptrap Cathedral peaked my interest. I first visited the cathedral on the school trip many years ago and I remembered a couple of my classmates walking into a secluded corner of the cathedral and scratching their names into the exposed stone work indoors. It didn't take me long to find this corner and, to my surprise their names were still there albeit a little worn. I smiled as I reminisced about these old days before carrying on.

Claptrap Cathedral had changed little over the years but there were a few new exhibits within that weren't there when I was a child. Things such as glass display cases of old coins and Medieval bowls were new as were displays containing stuffed animals and old clothing worn by people who lived in Claptrap many centuries ago. The stuffed animals fell into the same category as the waxwork dummies in Claptout-by-the-Sea's waxworks as they weren't exactly done by qualified taxidermists. Some of the pieces were truly horrifying as the animals appeared to have been caught for all eternity in their shocked final stare moments before death. Imagine what a moose would look like if a huntsman had pointed a gun at his face and he knew exactly what his fate was going to be and you had the look of most of the animals here! Elephants, cats and dogs all possessed an absolute look of pure terror and I had to move away before I started to have nightmares! More stuffed animals were present in another room and these ones had a mixed range of looks to their faces. Some of them looked constipated while others looked surprised. A dog was grinning maniacally as he (or she) looked at a tiger that looked like it had been lobotomised while a cat looked surprised at the sight of a winking polar bear! At the end of my jaunt through the cathedral I walked into the attractions gift shop and purchased more fridge magnets and postcards as well as a small ceramic model of the cathedral. I then left to find the village's other ye olde attraction — Claptrap Castle.

Claptrap Castle was your typical medieval castle — or at least it should be. A few years ago a team of archaeologists from the University of Scruff arrived in Claptrap to ascertain the date of the castle. For decades the locals were convinced that it was a medieval castle built around 1325 and showed historical records to prove that the castle was built around that time. Unfortunately, the archaeologists discovered that the historical records were fake — the work of somebody in the 1950s who wanted to get rich by claiming he had in his possession some documents that were 'centuries old'. The archaeologists first discovered that the documents were fake when it was discovered that the paper was written on notepaper that didn't exist prior to World War II! This set alarm bells ringing but the locals retaliated by saying that the castle was likely to still be genuine and the person in the 1950s just wanted to make some money out of an ancient castle. The locals however were soon horrified when the archaeologists discovered that the castle was also fake. It turned out to be the work of a Victorian bloke who saw himself as an antiquarian. Fragments of Victorian dishes were found amongst the foundations of the castle and even Victorian mortar was used in the building of the so-called medieval castle. It didn't help matters when the gargoyles which adorned the archway above the front door turned out to be effigies of Queen Victoria herself! It also didn't help matters when the original building plans were discovered in the hands of the person from the 1950s. It turned out that he was the great grandson of the person who built the castle! Ever since that day the castle has been billed as 'the only Victorian medieval castle in England!'

The admission price to Claptrap Castle was just as

reasonable as Claptrap Cathedral and I was soon inside the attraction. The interior of the castle looked like a genuine medieval castle and if you didn't know that it was fake you would think that it was over six-hundred years old. I tried to put the 'revelation' of its true history out of my mind and enjoy the castle for what it was but it wasn't easy when its tagline of 'the only Victorian medieval castle in England' was plastered on every display case around! The displays themselves weren't exactly helpful in disguising its history either as they contained Victorian-era dishes and cutlery as well as photos of how the Victorians lived. The owners of Claptrap Castle appeared to enjoy its new history and had even gone to great lengths to locate photographs of the castle being built! I looked at some of the photos of middle-aged men wearing flat caps and braces to hold up their trousers as they built the castle using stone that was brought from a company who demolished a genuine medieval castle several miles away. After perusing more kitchenware and also several Victorian coins I was just about to head into the gift shop when somebody who worked at the castle approached me. The bloke was dressed in Medieval clothing and was obviously hired as an actor to try and portray Medieval life. Unfortunately, the actor wasn't familiar with local accents and dialects and started off our conversation with, 'Ay up, me duck' in a Birmingham accent! I wasn't interested in talking to him so I did what I always did in such a situation — I pretended to be a German tourist! I knew a few words of German and could even put on a German accent of sorts and so started off with a few meaningless words spoken in my cod German accent. The actor looked at me with the same kind of surprised look as some of the stuffed animals in Claptrap Cathedral before walking off. As he did so I heard him say, 'Bloody foreigners,' under his breath!

I headed into the gift shop and brought a few fridge magnets, pens, pencils and also a bookmark with the castle's tagline written on it. I was just about to exit the shop when I noticed a lovely ceramic model of the castle. I purchased this and thought about how this would look nice next to my model of Claptrap Cathedral in a display cabinet I had at home. I then left and headed in the direction of the pub which I had seen Jack entering a while ago.

As I was walking towards the pub I noticed an open top tour bus parked by the side of the road. I walked up to it and read the fare prices printed in bright yellow writing on the side of the red coloured bus. £3 for a journey around Claptrap interested me and so I got on and sat on the top deck. The bus drew off and first it drove past the pub that Jack was in. At the moment we passed however he wasn't in the pub but rather standing outside with a cigarette in one hand and a stream of chat-up lines coming from his mouth aimed at a young woman standing near him also enjoying a cigarette. The bus then passed the cobbled high street and a few thatched houses before driving past Claptrap Cathedral. More thatched houses and cobbled streets followed including another gift shop which I had somehow missed (I took note of its location for future reference) before we drove past a field where a male and female cow were obviously enjoying each other's company! A few moments later I noticed Paul — the Golden Trip Coaches coach driver urinating behind a bush before we drove past Claptrap Castle. The journey only took about twenty minutes and soon I was back where I had first got on the bus. I quickly nipped off to the gift shop I had noticed and purchased yet more fridge magnets and pens before heading to the pub.

The Car and Hedgehog was a quaint little pub that retained the same look of pubs from over fifty years ago. I found Jack sitting at a table alone drinking a pint of lager and went down to sit with him.

'Did you visit everything then?' he asked as he took a sip of his drink.

'Yes, I did.' I smiled. 'I have a bit of a soft spot for these kinds of places. They have a kind of olde world charm about them.'

'The only thing that I like about these places are the pubs,' replied Jack as he took another sip.

'We've got another daytrip coming up soon to Cowshit and I'm looking forward to that one. Have you ever been to Cowshit?'

Jack shook his head. 'Nope,' he said, 'but I've been to one or two other villages around here before. There are quite a few villages in this area that end in the word 'hit' and although I've never been in Cowshit I've once stood in Dogshit.'

'Is that place any good?' I asked.

'What? Dogshit?' Came the reply followed by another sip of lager.

'Yes'

'It's okay,' Jack said, 'it's got a nice little pub in it but that's all I know. I went there a few years ago on a bender with a few mates. We went around several pubs in the surrounding villages with the intention of getting drunk and picking up a few birds! I tried to pick up one nice sort in one of the pubs only to discover she was a lesbian. It put me right off my drink as I watched her sitting in the corner of the pub with her girlfriend trying to suck each other's faces off!'

Me and Jack continued to talk for a short while longer and I treated myself to a pint of Roadkill Bitter which was drinkable but not spectacular. Afterwards we left the pub and headed back to where the coach had parked up. We still had about an hour or so before we left Claptrap and we both sat on a bench near to a small cafe where we drunk a cup of coffee each. Jack then piped up once more.

'This reminds me of a daytrip I went on about a couple of years ago,' he reminisced. 'There were no pubs in the village and I ended up sitting on a brick wall facing some public bogs drinking a cup of coffee for the entire daytrip!'

'Weren't there any shops to visit or any other places to go to?' I asked.

'There was a supermarket and one of those country clothing stores that you find in every one of these villages but nothing much else unless you wanted to buy postcards or fridge magnets!'

'Sounds like my kind of place then!' I quipped. Jack gave a slight chuckle at this as he had already twigged on that I was obsessed with buying these kind of trinkets but it was a kind of, 'yer, let's move on shall we?' kind of chuckle.

Eventually the coach arrived after it had driven off somewhere else shortly after we had departed from it. All of us got back on but unfortunately me and Jack were stuck behind a queue of elderly passengers who seemed to take their time boarding. When everybody had finally got on the driver did the customary headcount and then drove off. Shortly after hitting the road the driver spoke over the tannoy — minus his obligatory belch.

'While all of you were exploring the delights of Claptrap I had a few words with a fellow coach driver who was also doing a daytrip from Claptout-by-the-Sea to here today. He travelled along all of the main motorways and B roads and claimed he reached Claptrap a lot quicker. He then asked me why I chose to drive through all of the small villages rather than using the main roads and I told him the truth — I told that the motorways were always crowded and congested and it would take a lot longer as a result. To prove that I took the quicker path this morning I will now return to Claptout-by-the-Sea using these motorways and B roads and we will all see that it is the slowest route.'

Half an hour later we were back in Claptout-by-the-Sea.

There was still another hour before dinner and so I had another quick walk around Claptout-by-the-Sea. It was a nice day and the lovely weather relaxed me somewhat. I walked up to Rusty Pier and had a few goes on some of the slot machines before checking to see what time Bertie Dastard was on. The poster outside the pavilion said he was on stage at 8pm but I knew from experience that the listed start time was never the actual time the person started. I recalled another occasion a couple of years ago where I wanted to see a magician. All of the posters claimed that he was going to start at 6pm but by 7pm I was getting restless waiting for him to even set foot on the stage. Half an hour later I saw him walk in through the front doors of the bar whereupon he started to chat up some of the female bar staff as he leaned on the bar drinking a pint of lager. At 8pm he finally started and it turned out that his original assistant had walked out on him earlier that afternoon and he needed another assistant. This was where one of the bar staff came in and for the next half hour he was performing a few basic magic tricks while the bar girl turned magician's assistant was awkwardly trying to help him out which wasn't easy considering the small amount of time she had been given to rehearse. At 9pm the female assistant had to leave because her time was up at the venue and the bosses of the bar wouldn't pay her overtime so she left and the magician spent the next half hour recruiting a new assistant from the crowd eventually selecting a less than glamorous forty-five-year-old woman who was being carefully watched by her husband in case the magician tried anything funny with her! It then got out of hand when the magician asked his second new assistant to 'put her doves in his hands' whereupon the woman's husband sprang to his feet and gave the magician a right hook!

I sat down for dinner in the restaurant and observed the obligatory reactions of Mr and Mrs Stopwatch while on my table Everage and Norden were quietly finishing off their main course of pork and apple sauce which looked less like pork and apple sauce and more like a random bit of meat that somebody had vomited over! My Chilli Con Carne arrived and it looked a lot more appetising than the pork and apple sauce. I ate it in almost record time before finishing off with cheese and biscuits as Jack made his appearance. Mr and Mrs Stopwatch were furious that this young upstart was taking liberties with the timing system of the restaurant and showed it in their faces hoping that Jack would notice and apologise. He didn't however and played a game on his mobile while his meal arrived which made his esteemed tablemates even more furious! In what looked like a recreation of a silent movie Mr Stopwatch stood up with a look of thunder on his face and angrily threw his napkin down onto his empty plate before walking out of the restaurant followed closely by his wife! While all this was going on Jack hit a high score on the game he was playing as Mr and Mrs Sneer gave him a nasty look each! The entertainment in the restaurant appeared to be more entertaining than the entertainment in the bar afterwards!

After purchasing bingo tickets from the reception I sat down in the bar with a drink deliberately choosing a seat directly opposite Mr and Mrs Sneer. Suddenly an elderly woman approached me and asked if I would move.

'Why?' I asked to the woman who had now been joined

by another elderly woman.

'This seat is reserved for the young girl we're with,' the first elderly woman replied as she and her friend sat down on the table next to mine. Mr Sneer gave one of his trademark expressions to me and I reluctantly moved to another seat. Moments later a third elderly woman sat at the table I had vacated and I expected the other two elderly women to tell her to move because that table belonged to a young girl. It was then that I realised that the "young girl" that the two elderly women were talking about was in fact the third elderly woman who had sat down! If this woman was considered a "young girl" to these people I wondered exactly how old the first two elderly women really were!

Bingo started and I won the first game which prompted the by now expected reaction from the Sneers. Everage won the second game and it was the first time I actually heard her say anything all week even though it was nothing more than a mumble of the word 'house'! The third house also went to me and the Sneers were almost as furious as Mr and Mrs Stopwatch had been in the restaurant earlier. They weren't having any of this and quickly drank up their bitter lemon and tonic water before walking out of the bar. After they had walked out an elderly man snatched up the Sneers' bingo tickets and played the final game in the book. The tickets won both the line and the house and the elderly gent gratefully pocketed the winnings! I wasn't all that far behind the Sneers as there was no way I was going to sit through another cabaret act — this time a group who all looked like Buddy Holly clones!

Chapter 7
A Chance Encounter

Rusty Pier was only a short walk from the hotel and I took a leisurely stroll towards it taking in all of the other quaint seaside hotels and shops en route. The evening was nice and as the tide came in and the sky began to darken I wondered what to do around Claptout-by-the-Sea over the following two days where there would be no daytrips. A walk on the beach? A few hours in the amusements? Claptout-by-the-Sea didn't have a massive amount of things to do but it was nice for a break away from reality.

As I approached Rusty Pier, I noticed somebody who looked familiar. The person was a woman a little younger than me and was dressed in a knee-length blue dress with a short leather coat over the top. The woman had blonde hair and looked familiar but I couldn't remember where I had seen her. I walked a little faster to get a closer look of her face but that didn't answer my question. The woman then walked straight on past Rusty Pier and, rather than making myself look like some kind of stalker I turned off and walked into Rusty Pier towards the pavilion.

I paid a small entrance fee to get inside and watch Bertie Dastard and headed for the bar. I grabbed myself a pint of bitter and was just about to find a table when I noticed a bloke standing at the other end of the bar. The bloke was none other than Bertie Dastard himself and he was talking merrily to a couple of other punters laughing and joking with them. Bertie was wearing a bizarre multi-coloured jacket and black trousers and looked like he had applied a little bit of clown makeup to his face! That aside, I crept a little closer and listened in to what he was saying. Bertie was largely just telling jokes and I hoped that he wasn't spending his repertoire of gags at the bar before the event actually started. Some of the jokes were amusing but they were the standard seaside blue comedian jokes that involved mother-in-laws and women drivers! Bertie continued to chat to the couple of blokes for a few minutes longer before finishing off his glass of double whisky and slipping backstage. (The term 'slipping backstage' was actually quite apt as he pulled open a door leading to the backstage that was only visible to anybody leaning against the bar and promptly slipped over!)

I finished my first pint and ordered a second before taking a seat that commanded a good view of the currently empty stage. Bertie wasn't due to turn up for another half an hour which gave him enough time to sober up although he was no doubt in his dressing room drinking whisky straight out of a bottle! I thought I'd get in before time so that I was guaranteed a table by myself. Fifteen minutes later I was just about to finish my second pint and get up when I noticed the woman I had seen earlier. She brought herself a drink and then looked around for a table before approaching mine.

'Is anybody sitting with you?' she asked politely as she stood over me. I looked into her face which I thought was quite pretty and tried to recognise her but my skill at putting names to faces was bad.

'Er, no,' I said in reply as I pulled out a chair for her to sit on. The woman sat down on it and thanked me before putting her drink on the table. It was here that I decided to ask her where I had seen her before. She must be somebody who was at the same school as me or maybe at a former workplace because I was sure I recognised her.

'I recognise you from somewhere,' I said politely, 'what's your name?'

The woman smiled as she took a sip of her drink. 'You're not supposed to ask such personal questions to a lady you don't know but if you must know my name is Tracey Turner.'

I ran the name around in my mind for a few moments but it still didn't ring a bell.

'You still don't remember me do you,' she smiled, 'which I'm surprised, because you saw me quite recently, although that last time I didn't look quite so ladylike. I remember you.'

She said she didn't look quite so ladylike last time I saw her — she must have been somebody I worked with at one of the factories I've been employed with in the past. Tracey then smiled as she explained herself.

'I'm the bass player with the Six Pissed Dolls,' she said, 'I remember you sitting near the front at The Punk Establishment last night with your friend who appeared to be spending much of his time looking at my legs rather than listening to the music!'

I laughed as everything suddenly became clear. 'Jack is like that,' I replied, 'I bet he's already noted down the colour of your knickers in his head!'

'That wouldn't surprise me,' Tracey said laughing, 'I get a lot of people who only come to see the band so that they can see what I'm wearing. Every time I notice one of those kind of creeps, I just move away.'

I introduced myself and then offered to buy her a drink

before Bertie came on stage. She accepted and I returned moments later with two drinks. Over the course of the next hour we spent more time talking to each other than listening to what Bertie had to joke about. Of the fragments of entertainment I heard that Bertie came out with I remembered him telling the two punters at the bar earlier. The rosy-cheeked comedian was seemingly more drunk than earlier and he slurred many of his jokes which was more amusing than his actual act. After a couple of jokes mocking Irish people he tried a bit of magic which completely failed to work properly. After trying to make a whisky bottle appear from out of a large metal tube (I think he was so drunk he was confusing his drinking in the dressing room with his act) he walked, or rather fell off stage and stumbled towards the bar with a hobble!

Tracey was local to Claptout-by-the-Sea as were the other members of the band. I discovered quite a lot about her during Bertie's drunk performance and a bit more afterwards. She lived in a nearby town called Flooded Bridge and regularly travelled to Claptout-by-the-Sea to both perform and to get away from her normal day job as a secretary for an insurance company.

Bertie finished his performance at half past ten with neither of us remembering much of what he said — not that we could understand his slurred speech much anyway! We both left Rusty Pier just as night was setting in and walked together along the seafront like a couple of lovers before choosing to have a couple of drinks in a small pub called The Wreck where we exchanged phone numbers. After leaving the pub, I escorted Tracey to the hotel she was staying at for the next couple of days before returning to her own town. We then kissed seemingly by accident before she asked me what I was doing tomorrow.

'I'm not doing anything special,' I admitted. 'I've got two free days to do whatever I like before I embark on another daytrip. I was planning on just walking around here.'

'Why don't we go to a theme park nearby tomorrow,' Tracey then suggested, 'there's a lovely one just outside of Flooded Bridge that I always go to. I haven't been there with company for a few years now because my other friends are afraid of roller coasters and Ferris wheels and it would be nice to have some. What do you say?'

'That sounds great,' I smiled, as I kept the information about my fear of Ferris wheels from her!

'Excellent!' Tracey said in an excited tone of voice. 'I'll pick you up from your hotel after you've had breakfast tomorrow morning. Don't be late!' She then walked through the main doors of the hotel and was gone. I walked back to my hotel feeling happier than I had for quite some time. I went back to my hotel room and sat down with a cup of tea for a short while thinking of the night before reading a chapter of a book I had brought with me. After finishing my tea, I looked out of the window of the room and caught a quick glimpse of two stray cats fighting before choosing to get an early night. The early night was the most peaceful and relaxing night I had had on my holiday so far and even the bed collapsing during the night didn't ruin the atmosphere.

Chapter 8
A Day at the Fair

I woke early the following morning feeling just as great as I had done the previous night. When I had first booked this holiday I was sceptical about whether I would have a good time or not but now I was convinced that this holiday was the best I had ever been on. After going for an early morning stroll on the beach I returned to my room and awaited breakfast which I hoped would be just as entertaining as dinner the previous day. I wasn't disappointed and, as I ate my breakfast I watched Jack enter the restaurant, sit down and then almost immediately Mr Stopwatch stood up, threw his napkin on the table in a fit of rage and walked out followed closely by his wife. I then eyed up Mr and Mrs Sneer and, true to form, they shot Jack a vicious look each! Surely it wasn't going to be long before punches were thrown or seating arrangements were rearranged. The Stopwatch Family were clearly pissed off that Jack wasn't arriving for his meals early and had taken it upon themselves to be offended. It made me laugh and I carried on eating as Everage and Norden finished off their breakfast before slurping on a cup of tea each.

After breakfast I met up with Jack outside the hotel and we laughed about the antics in the restaurant. Suddenly, a member of staff approached us both and gave us some news.

'Hello,' the man said, 'I'm the deputy manager of this hotel and I've had a complaint from Mr Pratt sitting at the same table as you sir.' The manager looked at Jack as he said this before continuing. 'Therefore we have decided to switch Mr and Mrs Pratt with you, sir in the restaurant (he looked at me as he said this).' Jack then laughed and put a reassuring hand on the deputy manager's shoulder.

'I'm happy with this arrangement but why don't you just tell the pair of Pratt's to shut their traps?'

'I can't do that,' replied the deputy manager. 'Mr and Mrs Pratt are the parents of somebody who owns a rival coach company to the one you are travelling on and I think they've been placed on this trip as spies to see how bad this hotel and the coach company are compared to their son's holiday package. If anybody does anything untoward them then they will almost certainly report back and try and steal customers off this business.' The deputy manager then walked back inside as Jack put out the cigarette he was currently smoking and lit another one. I then told him about last night.

'You'll never guess who I met last night?' I said almost excited.

'Father Christmas? The Tooth Fairy?' retorted Jack.

'Better than that,' I continued, 'I met Tracey — you know, the bass player from the Six Pissed Dolls.'

'You mean the chick with the white silk knickers?' came Jack's expected reply.

'I wouldn't know about that,' I said, 'I wasn't the one perving up their skirts!'

'There's nothing wrong with having a healthy interest in women,' said my lecherous holiday companion.

'There is if it only resorts to looking up women's skirts,' I replied. 'Anyway, I met up with Tracey last night and we had a wonderful time together.'

'You mean you pinned her against a wall and unlocked her door?'

'Don't be silly,' I said, 'I met her and we spent a good few hours together and we're virtually an item now.'

'Ha, ha dream on,' retorted Jack, 'the Six Pissed Dolls are savvy punk chicks who will only go for guys like me!'

'Not likely,' I said, 'they don't particularly like people who are experts on women's underwear — especially the type of underwear that is currently in use!'

'Well, they certainly wouldn't go out with bores like you. I can imagine your perfect date — sit in a coffee shop sipping on a cappuccino each before you suddenly say "hey, I've got a good idea — let's go around to my house and play a game of Monopoly!"'

I was just about to defend myself when a small blue car pulled up outside the hotel and Tracey got out. Jack stood there aghast as she gave me a peck on the cheek, looked at him and smiled before we both got in her car and drove off. As we went down the road I saw Jack still looking dumbfounded, his cigarette hanging limply out of his mouth like a cowboy in a bad western movie!

The amusement park was in an area between towns and to reach it we had to travel through one or two of the small 'thatched cottage' villages. We travelled through one such village and had turned off down a short road only to discover that it was blocked. I craned my neck to see what was going on and discovered that an off road 4x4 vehicle had hit a parked car and the two respective drivers were on the roadside shouting at each other. When I looked at one of the drivers I couldn't believe who it was. It was our coach driver Paul and judging by the words he was uttering it was clearly him who had caused the accident in his 4x4! At the present moment we couldn't get through so I sat back and listened to the conversation between the Golden Trip Coaches' esteemed driver and the innocent car owner who had had his car dented by him!

'What the bloody hell do you think you were playing at driving down this road in a tank!' said the car driver.

'It's not a bleeding tank,' replied the coach driver, 'it's a four by four!'

'Alright then, what the bloody hell do you think you were playing at by driving a four by four down this road?'

'I was going for a little drive but I didn't think I'd encounter a car parked in the middle of the sodding road!'

'It wasn't parked in the middle of the sodding road! It was parked by the side of the road. Get some damn glasses before getting behind a steering wheel again!'

'I don't need glasses. I was driving perfectly well within my limits when I hit your mobile chicane!'

'I was watching you out of my bleeding window! You were driving on the footpath!'

'I was not driving on the footpath — I was driving on the bloody road!'

'You were driving on the footpath and also on people's front lawns! How else do you explain your tyre marks on my neighbour's front lawn?'

'I was avoiding a hedgehog in the middle of the road!'

'There ain't any hedgehogs around here. You killed the last one off last year when you ran over it before hitting Mr Jessops car!'

'That wasn't me — that was somebody else!'

'It was definitely you — I can remember you coming out

85

of your four-by-four last year and having a similar argument. If I remember correctly, you blamed a kid wearing a clown suit which distracted you!'

'It wasn't a kid in a clown suit — it was a kid in a gorilla suit!'

'Oh, so you do remember it then?'

'I wasn't even there so how can I possibly remember it?'

This went on for about half an hour before they were broken up by a community police officer. Tracey then backed up and took another route to the amusement park.

Fun Village Amusement Park was in a bizarre location for an amusement park. It was in the middle of an area surrounded by supermarkets and office blocks and the top of the Ferris wheel must have commanded an excellent view of people pushing shopping trolleys to their cars! Tracey explained that the amusement park used to be twice its current size but at some point it was cut in half and part of it was sold to developers who soon stuck a few supermarkets and office blocks on the site. She also explained that there used to be a couple of nice hotels around here also but alas they were also replaced by a car park and a supermarket.

After paying the twenty pounds for a wristband that was decorated in bizarre shapes that looked like a cartoon explosion we studied the map of the park we were given and headed to a roller coaster that was bizarrely called Deathtrap! The name didn't fill me with much hope but it didn't seem to bother Tracey or even any of the other people wanting to ride it. We got on and I seemed to be the only one who didn't enjoy it as much as everyone else. As the train trundled up the first climb I was certain that my seat felt loose as if a bolt or two was missing. It was obviously my mind playing tricks on me as it occasionally did when on a fairground ride that involved heights. Tracey, along with all of the other passengers thrust their arms in the air as Deathtrap dipped and climbed along its course while I clung onto the bar in front of me! I enjoy going on roller coasters but some I enjoy more than others and Deathtrap was one of those rides I didn't rate too highly.

We next went on a large carousel called The Cavalry which both of us would have enjoyed more had it not been for a little kid wearing a cowboy outfit and waving around a realistic looking toy gun. At one point the kid pointed the gun at another rider who almost fell off their horse in fright! Tracey then dragged me onto the large imposing Ferris wheel I first noticed when entering the park. Thoughts of Claptout-by-the-Sea's Ferris wheel and the boy jumping up and down flooded my mind but they were soon quenched by the thought of somebody being with me. Like all of the other rides in the park the Ferris wheel had a name and this one was called The Wheel of Death which, like the roller coaster, wasn't exactly an ideal name for a ride! Me and Tracey got on the wheel and the first rotation went smoothly but then the second rotation didn't go exactly as planned. I happened to look down into another one of the buckets and noticed the same boy from Claptout-by-the-Sea's Ferris wheel sitting there. 'Please don't jump up and down, please don't jump and down!' I said to myself even though the plea was aimed at the boy. Fortunately, he didn't but he did start to talk about loose nuts and bolts for some reason which caused me to look around my own bucket to see if there was anything loose! After I had been reassured that I was safe I concentrated on other things. I looked towards a nearby supermarket and watched as a husband and wife (I assumed they were husband and wife although I didn't know for certain) squabbled as they stood in front of the boot of their car in the car park. As far as I could work out they were arguing as to which order the shopping bags should go into the boot of the car and I watched as the man put one bag in the car before the woman squabbled with him and took the bag back out and put in a bag of her choice! On the tenth and final rotation of the Ferris wheel I watched the car drive off — their argument settled — I then noticed that they had left one of their bags of shopping on the ground which was then picked up by another shopper and put into their own car!

After the Ferris wheel we went on a few low level rides such as the dodgems cars which were called Destruction Derby, a slot car type ride called Dangerous Drives and an indoor tunnel of love type ride called Caves of Doom. It seemed that most of the rides in Fun Village Amusement Park had strange names that related to death or risks to people's lives and I wondered if the owners of the place were also the ones who designed the mascots for Rusty Pier and Claptout Pier. Tracey then suggested we have something to eat. The amusement park was full of fast food outlets and we chose one that served cheeseburgers. I had eaten most of my cheeseburger when suddenly a well-aimed dropping fell from the sky and onto my fries. I looked up and noticed a seagull hovering overhead. In a manner that would have pleased Mr Sneer and waved my fist at it before dropping the fries in a nearby bin. The offending seagull then landed and began to eat the fries! The damn bird was no doubt crafty and shat over my meal deliberately just so that it could eat it!

After the meal we carried on our jaunt around the park and went on a few more rides we had yet to try out as well as going back on some of the rides we had already tried. We returned to the Ferris wheel which made me feel a little queasy just looking at it from ground level but as soon as we sat down and the ride started I seemed to lose my fear of it. Maybe it was the fact that Tracey was hugging me and talking to me throughout the ride or maybe it was because that kid wasn't on it this time!

'Are you doing anything tonight?' Tracey then asked as the Wheel of Death went around for another rotation.

'No, why?' I asked.

'Because my band is playing tonight — we're at this pub in my home town called the Cat and Dog. It's a lovely pub and does a cracking Chinese meal some nights.'

'Sounds great,' I replied, 'I'm up for that — I enjoyed your last performance and I think I'll enjoy it even more now that I know you a bit better.'

Tracey giggled. 'Did you like my last performance because of what I was wearing or because of the music? It seemed like your friend only liked what was on show the other night!'

'He does like punk music,' I explained, 'but he likes looking up women's skirts even better! Can you believe that he even told me what underwear you were wearing!'

'Cheeky sod!' retorted Tracey. 'He clearly hasn't got a girlfriend.'

'I wouldn't know,' I explained, 'I'm only on the same coach tour as him and I know bugger all about his private life.'

'His private life no doubt includes looking up women's skirts. I bet he goes around wearing shoes with mirrored toecaps and spends his time printing off pictures of half dressed women from the internet!'

I laughed at this and suddenly became convinced that Tracey's assumption of Jack was correct.

'I must confess,' I then said, 'I'm not exactly a massive fan of punk music but when I saw your band, I did find myself enjoying it. The nice women were a bonus!'

Tracey giggled again and wrapped her arms around me before kissing me.

It was soon time to leave Fun Village Amusement Park because the place closed at 5pm and by about 4pm the place got a little empty and not much fun. We ended the trip by popping into a gift shop where I brought a few fridge magnets, pens and bookmarks as well as a gift for Tracey. She was looking at a large teddy bear with the amusement park's name on a t-shirt it was wearing and she admitted that she was in love with it.

'More in love with it than you are with me?' I asked.

'Of course not,' she giggled, 'but it comes a close second!'

I brought the toy and gave it to Tracey who hugged it and hugged me before we returned to the car.

We returned to Claptout-by-the-Sea a short while later and Tracey parked the car on a side road before we got out and took a walk along the beach. The evening was slowly drawing in and as we walked hand-in-hand we gazed upon the beautiful reddish-orange sky. We then gazed at the sea and I noticed in the near distance a small plop as if something had dropped into the water. I then looked towards the beach and noticed a man putting a catapult back into his pocket! We walked onwards and on towards the legs of Rusty Pier which were already part submerged in the water due to the tide slowly making its way inland.

Tracey took off her shoes and I did likewise and carried them before walking underneath Rusty Pier letting the water splash against our ankles.

'I feel like we're acting like a pair of love-struck kids,' giggled Tracey as she leaned against one of the legs of the pier.

'I know,' I replied smiling, 'I never expected to spend my holiday with a woman and I feel so excited whenever I'm with you.'

'Me too,' smiled Tracey, 'I only came here to perform in the band — not to fall in love but that's exactly what's happened. I haven't had a man in my life for quite a while now and I don't know how to act around them — I hope I haven't embarrassed myself too much?'

'No, you haven't,' I said. 'Come on, let's walk a little further before making it back. Let's make the most of this lovely evening.'

We walked almost a mile further on before heading back to my hotel. Once there Tracey agreed to meet me again straight after I had had dinner before driving off.

I sat down at my new place in the restaurant and observed Mr and Mrs Stopwatch not looking best pleased at Everage and Norden as they noisily ate their dinner and sipped on a cup of tea each. Due to the events that transpired this morning I forgot to ask about the chef's special so I settled for the usual muck that was served up on the menu. Jack then walked in and sat down opposite me on the table as Mr and Mrs Sneer shot him a nasty glance.

'So, how did your date with that hot chick go today?' was the first thing he asked.

'Fine,' I replied, 'we had a great time.'

'Have you boned her yet?' was his next question.

'Why do you always talk about sex whenever a woman is concerned?' I asked him as my plate of whatever it was supposed to be arrived.

'Because that's the only good thing about women,' he said, before asking me again. 'So, did you?'

'No, I didn't,' I said back, 'I've only known her about a day.'

'I bet you got caught in between her legs though didn't you? One lovely thigh either side of your face!'

'She was wearing trousers so that's unlikely and before you ask —no — she didn't take them off for me!'

I had obviously answered Jack's next question before he had the chance to ask it as he remained silent for a short while.

'When are you next seeing her?' he then asked which struck me as it wasn't a question about sex or certain female body parts. I decided to answer this question.

'I'm seeing her again after dinner. The band is playing at a pub where she lives and I'm going to see her play.'

'Make sure you get a front row seat,' Jack said, 'then you'll be able to see up her skirt when she comes on stage. I saw them last year and I spent the entire night looking at their knickers!'

I sighed and was just about to answer back when Mr Stopwatch stood up, threw his napkin down on the table in a rage and walked out of the restaurant closely followed by his wife!

'What happened there?' Jack asked.

'I don't know,' I replied, 'but I'd bet they were offended by the noisy eating of their new tablemates.'

'They're a miserable pair,' said Jack, 'I bet they are spies just as the deputy manager suspected. They most likely report everything back to their darling son like the good little parents they are!'

After dinner I hovered around the reception area of the

hotel for a few minutes until Tracey arrived. I watched as Mr and Mrs Stopwatch purchased bingo tickets before checking out the poster for tonight's 'entertainment'. According to the poster there was a duo on tonight called the Jones Brothers. They were both dressed in identical dark blue suits and white shirts and appeared to be some sort of clone of the Everly Brothers (although I didn't know that for certain because I had never heard any of their music or even knew what they looked like!) It was clear however that they weren't genuine brothers as they didn't even look remotely similar to each other. One was tall and clean shaven while the other was a short bearded man. The Jones Brothers had all the hallmarks of Arnold Schwarzenegger and Danny DeVito in the film Twins and this made me chuckle to myself which caught the eye of Mr Sneer who had just popped in to buy bingo tickets.

Tracey arrived as promised a few minutes later and she stepped out the car to show off her on-stage outfit of black T-shirt with a white lace vest-like top over it and a white lace and black satin mini skirt. She had also made her hair and face look a bit more punk but I could still recognise her.

'What do you think?' she asked smiling.

'Amazing,' I replied, 'Jack — the bloke who you keep calling "my friend" would be pleased.'

'He'd only be pleased to see me from the waist down,' laughed Tracey as we started to walk out of the hotel. As we did so I was sure that Mr Sneer uttered the words 'scruffy whore' under his breath at Tracey. I got into the passenger seat of Tracey's car as she got behind the wheel and started the engine.

Chapter 9
A Night on the Tiles

The pub was a nice small establishment — the kind with friendly locals and live entertainment on via a small stage set across one wall at the far end of the pub. Tracey stepped up on stage where the other band members were setting up their instruments and she introduced me to them.

'Hi, Emily,' she said to the lead singer. 'This is Dave — you know the bloke I met last night. He's come to see us tonight.'

Emily wasn't yet dressed up in her on-stage gear and looked like a regular pub goer in a black T-shirt and faded blue jeans. She also had yet to put on her 'punky' make-up and the lead singer looked more like a primary school teacher than a punk singer with her sparkling blue eyes and short dark hair. When I saw her the other night she appeared to have a blonde mullet with dark highlights so I assumed she wore a wig on stage. Emily smiled and seemed a bit too polite to be a supposed drunk punk band member and, out of curiosity, I asked her what she did as a day job.

'I'm a primary school teacher,' the lead singer replied which I thought was spooky considering that I thought she looked exactly like one.

'I saw the band the other night and you had a different hairstyle to what you have now — I'm assuming you wear a wig?'

Emily faced Tracey and smiled at her before saying, 'Your blokes a bit inquisitive isn't he?'

Tracey nodded without replying back. Emily then answered my question.

'Yes, I do wear a wig,' she answered, 'I don't think a punk hairstyle would go down well in a school. I'm supposed to be prim and proper not a wild child punk rocker!'

'Besides,' continued Tracey, 'it allows her to have any colour hair she wishes. I actually do up my hair but I wash it out again when it isn't needed. Emily here will most likely wear her pink wig tonight.'

Emily then shook her head. 'Not quite,' she replied, 'I've got a lovely blue one with green and blonde streaks in it. I trial fitted it earlier and I look so cool!'

One by one Tracey introduced me to the drummer Katie, lead guitarist Jenny, rhythm guitarist Liz and keyboardist Wendy — all of whom were either part dressed for the gig or not dressed up at all. This kind of set-up reminded me of an amateur wrestling match I saw whilst on holiday a few years ago where a Big Daddy lookalike helped construct the wrestling ring along with a Giant Haystacks lookalike — all of them dressed in dungarees!

I sauntered over to the bar and brought myself a pint of bitter and also a glass of tonic water for Tracey (she didn't want anything alcoholic prior to the performance which made the band seem they had chosen the wrong name when deciding on their moniker — but the Six Sober Women One of Whom was a Teacher didn't quite sound like a very good punk band name!) I sat down on a seat near the stage as the bar started to fill up and waited for the band to play. Once each of the members had set up their instruments they all disappeared backstage to get changed into their on-stage gear before returning about ten or fifteen minutes later dressed like the true punk icons they were.

One by one they ticked off all of the standard punk hits that I wasn't all that familiar with but vaguely knew of as well as inserting a few of their own songs for variety. After the forty-five session was over the girls all left the stage and popped to a small dressing room round the back of the pub before returning looking more like regular visitors to the bar including Emily who had returned to her primary school teacher appearance via a stint looking like Billy Idol after mistaking a can of spray paint for hair lacquer! Tracey however hadn't changed and sat with me still wearing her stage outfit asking of my opinion about the band as well as chatting about other things while a couple of roadies for the band (Tracey claimed they were boyfriends of Katie and Wendy) took away all of their instruments and amps and bundled them in a van in the pub car park. As we drunk our second alcoholic drink together, (Tracey was now on a glass of cider bizarrely called Appletizer) I asked her if she could sing herself because I had never heard her before.

'I can sing,' said Tracey, 'but there isn't any call for it in the band. I used to be the lead singer of another band a few years ago called Punk Off and I used to do a lot of karaoke in this pub as well but over the years I put it on the side-lines while I concentrated on the band.'

'You're happy with that arrangement then?' I asked.

'Sort of,' she replied, 'I do miss the days when I was the lead singer of a band but nothing lasts forever and I just accepted being a bass player when my previous band split up and I joined this one.'

'You should try out as a singer again,' I said, 'maybe as a solo singer this time. If your voice is anything as beautiful as you then you'll go down a storm.'

'Flattery will get you nowhere,' she replied as if she was still in her punk persona. I imagined her chewing on some gum while she said this whilst checking her nails to see if the black varnish hadn't worn off.

'It was worth a try,' I smiled.

'But who will support me?' she then asked as if unconvinced.

'I will,' I said holding her hand, 'you know I'll never desert you.'

'You need more than one person supporting an artist,' she replied, 'it would look funny if I was on stage singing a few songs while at the front of the stage there was you dancing and singing along to the music while everybody else sat at their tables drinking their pints thinking "who the hell is this weirdo!"'

'I'm sure I could put the word around,' I said finally, 'posters around town also help.'

Tracey then smiled. 'Thank you,' she said, before kissing me.

On the ride back to the hotel I told her that I had one further free day the following day and we could go out and look for any places around that would take her on as a soloist. Maybe some hotels would take her on if she put together a good routine and possibly even Rusty Pier would take a chance on her. Finally, she agreed to try out as a soloist and we agreed to meet again after breakfast tomorrow and maybe take in some of Claptout-by-the-Sea's other attractions such as a land train or even a tour bus that I had seen going around the resort. Tracey thought that was a good idea and with that Tracey dropped me off outside the hotel and waved to me as she drove back off presumably back to her home village of Flooded Bridge.

I had lost all concept of time with Tracey tonight and it was past midnight when I returned to the hotel. The main door was locked and I knocked on it to get someone to open it. There was no reply and so I knocked once more but this time a little harder. Still no reply and so the knocking turned almost into a banging which also received no reply. I looked around a little bit peeved that a thoroughly wonderful day had ended like this and decided to walk along the main road on the same side as the beach for a short while. The tide was in and the nearer I got towards the beach the colder the breeze was. I was only wearing a summer jacket because I didn't think I would be locked out of my hotel and, as such, I was feeling the almost icy sea air. Both piers were closed for the night and the lights that normally illuminated them in the darkness had been turned off leaving just a black shadow stretching out to sea that was only just visible in the night sky. Eventually I returned to the hotel and tried knocking again to get a reply but got nothing. All of the lights that normally shone through the windows were off so I assumed every guest had gone to bed including Jack. I then chose to sleep outside for the night which was not what I had planned but there was nothing else I could seemingly do. There was a small patch of grass outside the hotel ringed by a series of white tiles. The tiles however weren't quite white and looked more like a combination of cream and green and even had one or two cigarette ends crushed out on them. I settled down in a manner that I guessed a homeless person would and rested on the patch of grass which was surprisingly more comfortable than the beds inside the hotel!

Chapter 10
Enquiries and Investigations

It was Jack who found me the following morning. He had gone outside at about 6am for his early morning cigarette and noticed me sleeping on a small patch of grass outside the hotel.

'Good night last night I noticed,' he quipped, 'I take it you pinned her against the wall and gave her some!'

'I was locked out of the hotel and nobody would open the door,' I replied, 'but, yes it was a good night.'

'I was locked out last year,' Jack explained, 'It was on the final day I was here and all of the other days they had let me in when I knocked, but that night, they wouldn't let me in. I looked through the keyhole and there was nobody there at reception. My best guess was that the security guard was porking one of the female staff who were most likely still on site. I ended up sleeping rough by the side of the beach only to discover that that was the worst place to choose to sleep. I woke up the next morning soaked by the incoming tide and covered in seaweed!'

I laughed at this little anecdote and realised that my night of sleeping rough wasn't as bad as Jack's — assuming that is, his story was genuine. You could never tell with him!

At breakfast me and Jack talked about my night. He seemed to be quite fascinated with my relationship with Tracey but I had a suspicion that it was because he had his eyes on one of the other band members of The Six Pissed Dolls. My suspicions were confirmed when he uttered the words, 'Are any of the other babes in the band single?' I knew that two others had boyfriends so I guess that left just three other members. Jack begged me to ask Tracey and I agreed to do so but I did warn him that it might not get anywhere.

Me and Jack watched with fascination at the now expected entertainment of Mr and Mrs Stopwatch walking out of the restaurant in a fit of rage after Everage and Norden slurped their coffee and noisily ate their breakfast followed by the obligatory nasty look directed at me and Jack by Mr Sneer. After breakfast we both headed out of the hotel and waited outside for Tracey to arrive which she did about ten minutes later. Before I could say anything to her however Jack approached her car and started talking to her. He wasn't saying anything meaningful though and most of the stuff was just his usual chatter such as, 'Hi babe. Are any of the other gorgeous bits of stuff in the band single?' and, 'I bet you're walking like John Wayne this morning!' Tracey looked towards me puzzled as I got into the car and after I had explained what Jack meant she looked at him and decided to play tricks with him.

'Well, there is this one girl in the band,' she said, 'that can't keep her legs closed whenever she sees a fan!'

'Fantastic,' replied Jack, 'let her know that I'm interested and I'll show her a good time!'

'Will do babe,' said Tracey with a flutter of her eyelashes before driving off.

'Did you mean any of that?' I enquired once we had reached a safe distance away from the hotel.

'Don't be silly,' Tracey giggled, 'I've met creeps like him before. Jenny — you know, the lead guitarist in the band — is single but I doubt she'd want someone like him although she has gone out with worse in the past. Anyway, what do you suggest we do today?'

'I did say that we could try and scout around and see if we can try and launch a solo career for you — that's if you're still interested. We could also go on one of those tour buses that travel around here and see some of the sights.'

'Sounds good,' replied Tracey, 'but those tour buses aren't all sunshine and smiles though. Some of the stuff you see during the course of your journey isn't exactly the kind of stuff you'd write home about.'

'Don't I know it!' I smiled as I told her of my tour bus trip around Claptrap.

'There's also bad weather to contend with,' Tracey added, 'I went on a tour bus once and sat on the top deck of the open bus and no sooner had I sat down than it started to rain — hard!'

'I bet you were soaked,' I said almost giggling.

'Soaked?' replied Tracey, 'I was drenched! Your mate would have liked me because I bet he gets off on all of that wet T-shirt stuff!'

'It wouldn't surprise me,' I replied.

We then moved onto the subject of enquiring about her prospective solo career.

'So, you're definitely interested in launching a solo career then?' I asked as Tracey pulled down a side road.

'Of course, I am,' smiled Tracey, 'but I don't want to quit the band though — I'm still having fun with them.'

'Can you play any other instruments other than a bass?' I then said.

'I can play lead guitar,' she replied, 'but there's not much call for me to play that in the band because we already have two guitarists.'

'There might be some call to play it if you go solo,' I said.

Tracey parked the car in a car park near a shopping centre across the road from Rusty Pier, and we got out. On the backstreets of Claptout-by-the-Sea were a couple of small pubs and we went inside to enquire if they were interested in live music. One of them wasn't interested but the other was.

'What material do you have?' said the landlord who looked like a cross between Albert Steptoe and the Hunchback of Notre Dame. We were silent for a moment. We had spent so much time thinking about carving out a solo career for Tracey that we hadn't even thought about what material she could do. Suddenly Tracey spoke up.

'I'm a singer and guitarist who does all kind of punk and rock music.'

'Do you do rock and roll?' asked Steptoe.

'Only if I put a sort of punk sound to it,' Tracey said.

'I'm not interested in punk,' said Steptoe presently, 'and if that's all you can do then I'm not interested.'

As we left the pub I said, 'These oldies only seem to be interested in the music of ye olde times! I bet if an Elvis Presley impersonator walked into that pub he'd get a gig instantly.'

'Presley impersonators always amuse me,' replied Tracey. 'They all seem to model themselves off his 1970s image when he was the patron saint of double cheeseburgers! Most of them look like a cross between Bernard Manning and Alvin Stardust!'

We left a third pub disappointed but it wasn't the end. There were other pubs around the area but Tracey suggested that we sort out the material first before trying to get any gigs.

I suppose she was right — after all, she knew more about the live music business than I did.

After walking through the shopping centre we were about to go back to the car when I noticed a coach parked nearby. Upon further inspection I noticed it was one of Pratt's coaches and to my surprise I noticed the driver standing in front of the door speaking to none other than Mr and Mrs Stopwatch.

'That's an elderly couple from the hotel,' I whispered to Tracey as I stepped a little closer.

'So what!' Came her reply.

'A few people who work at the hotel are convinced that they've been planted on the coach holiday just to spy on what goes on and to report back to their son who owns the Pratt's coach company. The bloke they're talking to is most likely their son.'

'So what are you planning to do?' asked Tracey, 'spy on them while they spy on you?'

'Yep!' I said proudly.

'Cool,' replied Tracey, 'I like a good mystery!'

Me and Tracey stood behind a wall and listened to the couple and their son talk.

'So what happened yesterday then dad?' asked the coach driver who, like the Golden Trip coach driver was obviously a lover of food but a hater of diets.

'The staff are useless,' said Mr Stopwatch, 'and the guests likewise. Most of the guests are ignorant. We used to sit at a table in the restaurant with a young lad who spent more time on his telephone than eating his meal. He also came in late instead of at the correct time. It's a good job he isn't in the army — they wouldn't stand for such an ass as him!'

'So he was on his mobile and came in late,' said the driver

as he took notes down in a notebook. 'Anything else?'

'This young whippersnapper now shares the table with another young ass who also comes in late. He also seems to be spending a lot of time with a woman lately who isn't a paid member of the tour. I wish people on this tour would only socialise with other people on this tour and spend more time enjoying the relaxation of the hotel rather than going out. I wouldn't be surprised if this other young bloke and that woman are disgracing themselves on the beach late at night!'

'What an absolute bastard!' said Tracey, 'what you and I do with our time isn't of their concern. How dare he invent such silly stories about us!'

I laughed as I put my arm around her. 'Just laugh it off,' I replied, 'most of the oldies at the hotel are a bit strange. Anyway, this spying lark would make a cracking song!'

Tracey smiled. 'Yes, it would,' she said back. 'I think I could make something out of it!'

After the Pratt's coach had driven off and Mr and Mrs Stopwatch had popped into a shop — no doubt to buy next week's groceries — we headed to the beach rather than back to the car as we had first planned. It was a lovely day and we walked barefoot along the beach but we soon put our shoes back on when we noticed a dog running around on the sand. We then discovered that the dog belonged to the bloke with the catapult so I at least was moderately relieved that we wouldn't be stepping in anything we didn't want to!

The beach was packed and there were many people there. Kids were running around while their parents went to sleep and even the Ferris wheel kid was there drawing pictures in the sand with a stick. I was going to ignore him but then I noticed that he was drawing a picture of a Ferris wheel and was using seashells he had found as the 'buckets' on the ride. When the picture was complete he then took one of the seashells and simulated it falling off the Ferris wheel before crashing to the ground accompanied by a crashing sound made by him! Images of my first ride on the Ferris wheel flooded my mind momentarily before Tracey spoke to me.

'Look at all of those radio-controlled planes,' she said as she pointed to several planes and helicopters flying around overhead. I looked at them and then looked at the people controlling them who all seemed to be getting on well with each other...... until one plane crashed into another! As the debris fell to the ground the controller of one plane walked up to the controller of the other plane and started to argue with him!

'What the hell do you think you're playing at you blind Kamikaze loon!' one said.

'It was an accident,' said the other.

'Accident!' said the first bloke 'ACCIDENT! That was no accident. That was deliberate! You did that because you were jealous that your ex-missus is now going out with me!'

'That's got nothing to do with it.' Came the reply. 'Anyway, it was my twin brother who you stole his missus off!'

'You don't have a twin brother!' shouted the first man.

'Yes, I do — he's over there look.' The second man then pointed to a bloke behind the first man. The first man turned around to look for whoever the second man was pointing at and when he turned back around he discovered that the second man had done a runner! The first man was seething and was just about to walk over to the debris of his plane when Catapult Man's dog beat him to it and urinated over the debris. The first man then started an argument with Catapult man as the Ferris wheel kid drew a picture of two planes crashing in the sand followed by another picture of a dog defecating over the wreckage!

Me and Tracey found a quiet part of the beach and sat down on it watching the tide wash the beach several metres in front of us. As we watched the waves I thought of an idea.

'How about you become a comedy singer?' I suggested.

'A comedy singer?' she replied, 'I don't know the first thing about writing comedy songs.'

'It's not all that hard,' I said, 'ever since I've been here at Claptout-by-the-Sea I've found several things that have amused me. You have too. The Pratt's coaches' incident and the radio-controlled planes argument are just two such examples. I'm no good at writing comedy stuff out of nothing but I can write loads of stuff if I'm given inspiration.'

'If you're that good you should write a book and get it published.' Tracey said.

'I suppose I could but I'm afraid I'll get negative feedback from people who leave comments on shopping websites that are named after South American rainforests!'

'If you write a few songs for me,' Tracey then suggested, 'I'll give it a go.'

'I'll go along with that,' I replied before we both dropped back onto the beach and lay down soaking up the sun for a full hour.

We had planned to spend a bit longer on the beach but then the two radio-controlled plane operators who had argued bumped into each other and started to argue once more. The first bloke said something along the lines of, 'you trained that dog to piss all over the wrecked planes didn't you?' before me and Tracey left.

Just as we were about to head towards the waxworks for a first visit as a couple (and potentially some inspiration for another song) we noticed one of Claptout-by-the-Sea's tour buses parked nearby.

'Let's get on that,' I suggested, 'we did think about going on one of those earlier on.'

'Why now,' smiled Tracey, 'it's a nice day and it should be a great sightseeing tour if we sit upstairs.'

We stepped onto the bus and I paid £4 each for both of us for a return ticket and took a seat on the top deck. The bus set off and we pointed out things such as the Ferris wheel and also more arguing on the beach from the RC plane operators and were just about to enjoy the nice quiet ride when a two young blokes starting talking a few seats back from us.

'I got a new job yesterday,' said one.

'Oh yeah,' said the second, 'where?'

'At the same place where Pube-like works.'

'Who's Pube-like?'

'You know,' said the first, 'he's the bloke whose hair looks like a thatch of pubic hair so we call him Pube-like.'

'Does he mind?'

'Well, he hasn't hit me yet!'

The conversation went on for about ten minutes and I found out that the first bloke was working in a cold meat factory where the workers have a habit of dropping the meat onto the floor and then subsequently picking it back up and putting it back into production as if nothing had happened to it. I blanked out bits of the conversation and concentrated on the sights as the tour bus went along back streets showing me amusement arcades I hadn't seen before and even another attraction called Claptout House which was billed as a kind of dungeon-themed place. Tracey had also noticed Claptout House and suggested we have a look around it at some point which I thought would be a good idea. I would be hoping that it was a genuinely frightening experience where the girl (Tracey in this case) would be scared and wrap her arms around me to protect her but I had a feeling that it would be about as frightening as a kid wearing a white sheet and saying, 'boo'!

As the tour bus threaded its way through some of the back streets, I noticed the Pratt's coach driving off somewhere and also Mr and Mrs Stopwatch just exiting a supermarket with two bags of groceries. It then drove past a pub where Jack was sitting in the beer garden with a pint of lager on the table and trying to chat up a woman — and failing before driving past a couple of crazy golf attractions and another amusement arcade. It finished by driving past the two piers and dropping us back off at the stop where we had first boarded. The two blokes who sat behind us got off the bus first and they were greeted by another young bloke with out-of-control wiry dark grey hair.

'Hey, Pube-like,' said the first bloke, 'what you doing here?'

'Don't call me Pube-like,' said the third bloke angrily who then promptly gave him a right hook to floor him!

We walked along the main road for a short while before visiting the waxworks. It was the second time I had visited this 'attraction' but the first time I had visited it with Tracey and the first time Tracey had visited it as an adult.

'My parents used to take me here regularly,' she remembered. 'I don't know why — maybe they just wanted to scare me! The first time I visited this place I thought it was one of those novelty dungeon attractions that are springing up all over the place at the moment. I think it took me about three years to realise that the waxwork I thought was of Frankenstein was actually of a famous pop singer!'

I laughed as we observed all of the waxworks and laughed at who they were supposed to be. We found one waxwork of a footballer who looked like a Canadian Bigfoot hunter and got another visitor to take a picture of us with our arms around the bearded footballer who, to my best knowledge, had never grown facial hair in his life! After posing for a photo of what looked like Frankenstein sitting at a writing desk wearing a pair of spectacles and writing a novel we left the waxworks.

This photo opportunity had given us the bug and we spent the next two hours getting other holiday makers to take pictures of us in various locations. The beach became the next victim and the photographer caught Catapult Man in the background disposing of his pet's waste and another of the two radio-controlled plane blokes arguing in the background. More pictures were taken of us in the aquarium and even outside The Punk Establishment and the arcades. Finally, we descended upon Rusty Pier where we took the last of our photographs together before the rain came down! Both me and Tracey ran as fast as we could back to her car which was a fair distance away and stayed there for a while as we caught our breath. After our energy had returned we shared a passionate embrace before Tracey asked if I would skip dinner at the restaurant tonight and have dinner with her at a nice restaurant somewhere.

'What would you rather have,' Tracey said, 'dinner with a load of oldies — some of which are nosey little bleeders or dinner with me at a nice restaurant?'

I had to give it to her — she certainly knew how to persuade me!

Chapter 11
Dinner with George

Tracey dropped me off at the hotel as soon as it had stopped raining. While I changed into a nice shirt and trousers she went back to her house to change as well as wet clothing on a woman might have some appeal to Jack but not for the proprietor of a restaurant. While I waited in the reception for her I took a glance at tonight's hotel entertainment. They had a band on tonight called the Soul Survivors which I guessed was a hint at what kind of music they specialised in but could also hint at them being the last remaining people who genuinely enjoyed their music! As I studied the poster Jack came down into the reception.

'Hi,' he smiled, 'did you enjoy your day with your bit of crumpet today?'

'I did, yes,' I replied, 'but I doubt she would like to be called "a bit of crumpet".'

'All girls love being called names like that — look I'll show you. There's a new girl behind the reception desk today,' he gestured towards a young woman in reception with his head, 'and I'm going to have her eating out of my hand in no time!'

'You really think so do you?' I said sceptically remembering his failed attempt at the pub earlier which he didn't know I knew about.

'Oh yes,' he smiled, 'she'll be taking her knickers off and

passing them to me in no time!'

I watched as Jack sauntered up to the reception desk with a corny ladyboy kind of walk and looked at the girl behind the counter. She looked like she was only nineteen but I had to admit she was quite good-looking. She was too young for my liking but Jack didn't seem to bother. I actually didn't know how old Jack was but I was sure he was at least ten years older than this girl who looked barely legal to drink alcohol!

Jack leaned on the desk and smiled at the girl.

'Hi babe,' he said, 'fancy a great time tonight? There's a lovely bar we can go to where we can have a few drinks but if you prefer to have a good time in private we can go up to my room and give you a good ribbing! What do you say?'

The girl looked at Jack and then looked at me as if to clarify what language he was speaking in before giving her reply. 'I don't date weirdo's,' she said in the kind of tone of voice that I imagined would be the audio equivalent of text messaging, 'besides, I already have a boyfriend. My daddy owns this hotel and I don't think he would be happy if I was to abuse my privileges here.'

'I wouldn't mind if you abused my privilege,' returned the self-styled lothario, 'It's ten inches long and enjoys the company of sexy ladies such as you!'

The girl looked at me again as if to clarify before giving her own answer.

'I — Don't — Date — Weirdo's,' she replied leaving a space between each word so that Jack could digest each one easily. Jack was annoyed at this and made his displeasure quite vocal.

'Suit yourself then,' he said as he walked away, 'she's most likely bi-sexual,' he whispered to me as he walked past.

Once he had gone the receptionist looked at me and smiled.

'What do you see in him?' she asked.

'Nothing,' I replied as I saw Tracey's car draw up outside the hotel.

The queue for the restaurant soon built up and I was fortunate to be near the hotel exit as Tracey appeared. She looked wonderful in a smart, long, dark blue dress and small white cardigan and even Jack was impressed. He was outside having his obligatory cigarette and had only walked back into the hotel just as Tracey did. As she walked past him he gave her a wolf whistle. I took Tracey's hand and we both walked out of the hotel as Mr and Mrs Sneer stood in the restaurant queue following us with their eyes. Again, I heard Mr Sneer mutter something under his breath as we left and I was certain this time he was referring to Tracey as some kind of woman who enjoys gangbangs with me and Jack!

As we drove off I asked Tracey which restaurant she had in mind.

'It's an Indian restaurant,' she answered, 'you know – all curries and naan bread.'

'And farting,' I replied back, 'I went to an Indian restaurant once and there were about eight blokes all sitting around a table competing in a farting competition! I don't know who won but the contest sounded like a badly tuned brass orchestra!'

Tracey laughed. 'This one is quite nice,' she said, 'the place is for the more refined guest and they don't allow the wind section into the place! You might actually like it.'

The restaurant Tracey had chosen was a nice large building in the nearby village of Little Drainage — a village notable for regular floods during rainstorms. The restaurant was owned by a local entrepreneur called Josh Rogan who owned several Indian restaurants around the Claptout-by-the-Sea area. Me and Tracey walked inside and were soon seated at a table for two in the middle of the restaurant. As we waited for the starters to arrive Tracey started to talk about Mr and Mrs Stopwatch.

'I still can't get over how those two old people — what were their names — Mr and Mrs Pratt were talking about us to their son who owns that coach firm.' Just as I was about to reply a man sitting on the next table with a woman — who I presumed was his wife spoke to us.

'Are you talking about the Pratt family?' he said in between mouthfuls of curry. 'The ones who own the Pratt's coach company?'

I nodded. 'Yes,' I answered, 'why do you ask?'

'I used to work for them,' the man replied before swallowing his food, 'I used to be one of their coach drivers. John Pratt runs the business now but his father, Stan, used to run the company until her retired a few years ago and handed the reins over to his son. I couldn't stand Stan — he was always moaning and complaining about everything and always looked at his wristwatch whenever a driver turned up late or turned up on time for his shift. Even when he didn't have a watch on he was still looking at his wrist!'

Tracey giggled. 'Dave here is on a rival coach holiday in Claptout-by-the-Sea at the moment and he's staying in the same hotel with the elderly Pratt's. He's told me they still look at their watches whenever somebody comes into the restaurant late.'

'That doesn't surprise me,' said the man who introduced himself as George Brewer. 'I bet they're also reporting back on the hotel activities to their son as well!'

'How did you guess!' I replied, 'I caught them doing just that this morning!'

'Most likely trying to bring down the rival coach company from within,' said George.

Our starters arrived, and as we ate, we continued to talk to George who seemed like a nice individual — certainly much nicer than the elderly guests at the hotel. George explained that he left Pratt's shortly before the elderly Pratt retired and now he works as an entertainment manager at a club nearby.

'Are you looking for any entertainment for your club at the moment?' I suddenly chipped in.

'I'm always looking for entertainment,' he replied, 'why do you ask?'

'Because Tracey here is a bassist in a band but she's looking to start a solo career. She hasn't got any material as yet but we're both hoping to get things sorted out sometime soon.'

'What band are you in?' George asked.

'The Six Pissed Dolls,' replied Tracey.

'You're in the Dolls?' George said seeming slightly stunned. 'I've seen them play a few times — they're actually quite good. I've tried to book them before but they seem to be quite popular.'

'Yes, we are,' said Tracey, 'we've been doing gigs almost once a night recently all over the place so you could say we're popular.'

'I'll tell you what,' offered George, 'get some material together and I'll hire you if you can find time away from the band.' He then took a business card out of his jacket pocket and handed it to Tracey. 'My name, number and address of the club is on there — make sure you give me a ring when you're all sorted.'

'Thanks,' Tracey said smiling — clearly delighted. 'I will do.'

Both the meal and the company were excellent at this place and after we had paid we left and headed for a local pub that Tracey had recommended. We stayed here for a while and as we walked back to the car I mentioned to her about the daytrips laid on by the coach company tomorrow and asked her if she would meet me at any of the places.

'I can't I'm afraid,' she said sadly, 'I've got band practice all tomorrow morning and a gig tomorrow night so I can't even though I'd want to. We can certainly meet up again when you come back from the trips because I'm sure I'll have some spare time then. Maybe you can even watch the band tomorrow night if you're interested.'

'I'd love that!' I exclaimed as we got into the car.

On the way back to the hotel we took a detour past George's club just to see what it was like. The outside was fairly smart and didn't seem to attract the kind of ruffians that other clubs seemed to attract. A large bouncer was standing outside wearing the usual black suit and white shirt that most of the kind seem to wear and his imposing stature appeared to frighten off even the most hardcore of drunks. We parked the car nearby for a few minutes and watched the club just to gauge if it really was the ruffian-free establishment we thought it was. Suddenly, a drunk man started to walk past presumably from a pub just down the road. The bouncer looked at the drunk who presumably had a barmy notion of trying to get into the club and snarled at him. The drunk looked at the bouncer, straightened himself up and then walked across the road to carry on walking on the other side! We then drove back off to the hotel.

After Tracey had dropped me off and had driven off, I banged on the locked up front door and was surprised that they let me in tonight unlike the previous night. I headed straight back up to my room and got into bed... and then got back out again to sort out the collapsed bed before getting back in again. Before I drifted off to sleep I thought about travelling to Cowshit and then to Boggy Sands tomorrow and wondered if the coach driver would take us on another detour like he did last time. I expected him to travel somewhere miles away from the destination before travelling back through Claptout-by-the-Sea and then onto Cowshit! I'd never been in Cowshit before but I expected it to be another rural village that would delight the oldies on the coach I had however visited Boggy Sands once or twice before and I hoped that it had been restored to its former glory since the last time I had been there. My suspicions however were that the former popular holiday resort had been left to rot — partly due to Claptout-by-the-Sea's increasing popularity and that visiting it would be like visiting a car scrap yard that had once been a thriving car dealership in years gone by. It kind of made me sad that some British holiday resorts had gone from being a popular summer holiday getaway to somewhere people would avoid in just a matter of years. Even Claptout-by-the-Sea isn't as good as it used to be according to old pictures I had found on the internet prior to me coming here.

Chapter 12
Caught Up in Cowshit

I woke up early the following morning to the now obligatory sunshine filtering through the hole in the curtain. I washed, shaved, showered and then walked downstairs to catch some of the early morning air. Unsurprisingly Jack was already up and outside smoking a cigarette. Judging by the smouldering butt that had been docked out on the footpath in front of him I guessed he was on his second one.

'Hiya mate!' he exclaimed. 'Looking forward to the trips today?'

'I certainly am,' I replied, 'but it's just a shame that Tracey has got band practice today and can't come along.'

'That's a likely story,' Jack smirked, 'girls who are as hot as her normally use excuses like that to ditch one bloke and go jumping into bed with another!'

'She isn't like that,' I protested, 'I've known her long enough now to know she's not that way inclined.'

'Oh really?' Jack said as he dropped his cigarette and stubbed it out with his foot. 'I bet there are a load of men who've seen her knickers — and I don't mean they've seen them by getting a front row seat at one of her gigs!'

'I wish you'd stop talking like that,' I said, leaning against the side of the hotel. 'You seem to talk non-stop about sex. If a woman doesn't like you it means she's a lesbian or bi-sexual and if a woman won't hop into bed with you on the first date it means she's a lunatic or something like that!'

'Well, she would have to be,' replied Jack, 'no woman can resist my massive shlong!' He then walked back into the hotel while I took a walk down the seafront.

Breakfast was still about another hour away and I spent the time spending some more cash in the arcades. After winning over two-hundred tickets at Rusty Pier I tried out a motion simulator ride. I slipped a pound coin into the slot, sat back in the seat and selected a ride called 'Wild Gold Mine'. I had expected an experience where I was seemingly riding in a runaway mine cart as it rattled along uneven and broken train lines in an underground mine but what I got was some kind of weak ride where I was sat in a mine cart being pulled by a miniature train driven by some swivel-eyed loony who looked like your stereotypical gold miner complete with a long grey beard tinged with tobacco stains and about four unclean teeth! I've been on better motion simulators before and this one didn't even compare to any of them! I then checked on all of the other 'rides' listed on the main menu of the ride and if I had looked through these first I could have saved myself a quid! Other ones included a ride on a toy train through a giant toy box, a go-kart ride around a largely boring track and finally a ride called 'the Teacup Ride of Doom'! According to the demo it was one where you were placed in one of those kids cups and saucers rides and it came off its mounting points and starting spinning on a pre-arranged track through a small amusement park! My own subconscious can think of more dangerous 'rides' when sitting on a Ferris wheel than the makers of this ride can!

After the motion simulator I tried a couple of more slot machines but was winning almost nothing. Suddenly I heard some bloke shout, 'Yay! Jackpot!' followed by the sound of lots of coins rattling out of a machine and into a metal tray. I turned around to see who it was but when I did find the person it turned out that he wasn't playing on a slot machine at all. He had put some money into a change machine and the machine had dutifully done its job by exchanging his pound coin (or whatever amount of money he had put in) for a load of two pence pieces! This then reminded me that I had yet to have a go on one of the 'penny-pusher' machines in any of the arcades yet. These simple child-friendly machines are the grand-daddies of seaside amusements and as a kid I could never stay away from them whenever I was on holiday with my family. On this holiday however I had pretty much shunned them in favour of the ticket producing slot machines. I reached into my pocket and found a few two pence pieces before inserting them into a machine based around Elvis Presley. A large overweight-looking Presley model was positioned on a rotating axis on the top of the flat circular machine and every now and then it would gyrate as if dancing. Music also accompanied the 'dancing' and I'm sure that the music playing should have been one of his hits but it wasn't. I can only assume that the music tape that had been inserted into the machine was the wrong one because every time the Presley model gyrated he did so to the tune of Chirpy, Chirpy Cheep, Cheep! I lost all of my spare two pence pieces on this machine alone and decided that this was a good enough excuse to leave.

As I walked back to the hotel I admired my surroundings. The old hotels neighbouring the new hotels, the cafes, the restaurants and thinking that my holiday would soon be over. I always seemed to feel this way near to the end of the holiday and I can remember when I went away last year, I got up early in the morning on the final day — five o'clock I think it was — just so that I could look out to sea one last time. I leaned against a metal fence separating the promenade from the steps leading to the beach and sighed. I think I even had a tear in my eye because I knew I would never be here again — at least not for a while anyway. The same would no doubt happen this year as well. For all of the faults that the hotel has to offer and all of the dubious people who walk along the beach Claptout-by-the-Sea has been good. There is no such thing as a bad holiday because even the bad ones make memories that you will remember for a long time. This then got me thinking. What if I never saw Tracey again after this holiday was over? Maybe our relationship is just one of those throwaway holiday romances that people have before returning to normality. Maybe Jack was right in saying that she has found somebody else because my holiday is almost over and I'm no longer needed.

No. That can't be it.

When I walked back into the hotel I was met by the same deputy manager who had confronted me and Jack a couple of days before regarding the restaurant seating arrangements.

I had a feeling this had something to do with Mr and Mrs Stopwatch again.

'We've had a complaint from Mr and Mrs Pratt again,' informed the deputy manager. 'They're not happy sitting on the same table as Mr and Mrs Sidebottom so we have decided that you and Mr Elliot will sit with Mr and Mrs Sidebottom while Mr and Mrs Pratt will take up their original table but this time without any company.'

'That would suit them down to a tee,' I said. 'The pair are the most anti-social old biddies I have ever met!'

'I wouldn't say that, sir,' replied the deputy manager, 'if they're listening, they will report back to their son's coach firm and we could find ourselves with bad reviews on the internet.'

'I couldn't care less,' I replied, 'they're the ones causing the trouble and making problems for everybody else.'

'That may be,' replied the deputy manager, 'but we have to keep them sweet — for our own welfare.'

With that the deputy manager walked away as I pondered the new information I had discovered in the form of Everage and Norden's real names and also Jack's surname which he had neglected to tell me thus far. All I needed now was to find out the names of Mr and Mrs Sneer and I had won my first game of Unhappy Families!'

As usual I walked into the restaurant at my usual time and sat down at the same table as Everage and Norden while Mr and Mrs Stopwatch were enjoying their own company at their original table. Jack then walked in and sat at the same table as me and we ordered our breakfasts. While we waited I watched the Stopwatch couple and anticipated some other complaint they would manufacture out of thin air.

I wasn't disappointed!

Mr Stopwatch ran a solitary finger down one of the restaurant windows that his table was up against, looked at his finger and then wiped it on the tablecloth! He then repeated the process with five other sections of windows before tutting loudly. After he had eaten breakfast he walked out of the restaurant in a slightly more dignified fit of rage than he had previously displayed disappearing from my vision as he did so. I suspected he was going to complain about the cleanliness of the restaurant windows to the deputy manager which would no doubt result in another table change for dinner later this evening. Breakfast and dinner was now starting to turn into a game of musical chairs for the pair of Pratt's and people such as me and Jack were on the receiving end of it! If what I suspected was true then they would be relocated to a table in the centre of the restaurant for dinner where there were no windows which would end up with another innocent couple being dragged into their complaining!

After breakfast Jack and I walked outside the hotel and waited for the coach to arrive for the trip to Cowshit. While Jack was getting through his second cigarette Tracey turned up in her car which surprised me.

'I just thought I'd come and wish you a great day before I go off for band practice,' she said.

'Thanks,' I replied, 'are you not going to turn up at Boggy Sands or Cowshit sometime during the day?'

'I might turn up at Boggy Sands later on,' she said, 'it just depends how band practice goes.'

'I didn't actually expect you to even turn up to see me off today. I thought you were going to go straight to band practice.'

'I've got a bit of spare time,' Tracey confirmed, 'but not much so I'll just stick around to see the coach leave and then I'll be off.'

Tracey then drove to a small parking area near to the hotel to park the car and walked back to the hotel entrance where we stood talking for the next ten minutes until the coach arrived. Just before I boarded the coach Tracey gave me a quick kiss and then said, 'I'll see you later.'

'Is that it?' I said with a smile, 'nothing more romantic?'

'I'm a punk chick,' Tracey smiled, 'punk chicks don't go waving their hands in the air like loved-up schoolgirls and then say stupid stuff like "love you, darling! I'll miss you!"'"

Once everybody had boarded the coach the driver closed the door, did a headcount, belched and then started the engine.

The coach started off and was on the road for a full twenty minutes before it drove past the Josh Rogan Indian restaurant me and Tracey visited the previous night. I found this odd but not all that surprising from this coach driver. It had only taken Tracey about three minutes to reach the restaurant in her car which suggested the coach driver was going on another detour! Another twenty minutes and several thatched house villages later we were on the outskirts of Cowshit. We passed the signpost saying, 'You are now in Cowshit,' before the coach started to make funny noises. It started to splutter and then slowly grind to a halt as the driver pulled to one side. The now familiar belch echoed over the tannoy before the author of the belch spoke up.

'We appear to be in a bit of a dilemma,' said the driver, 'I forgot to fill the coach up with fuel this morning and now it seems we're out of gas! I'm going to have to drop you all off here and ring the company for a replacement coach or a new tank of gas and pick you up in a few hours' time. The town square of Cowshit is just one mile up the road ahead and there you will find gift shops and tourist information centres. I will pick you up from the market square when everything is up and running again!'

The driver then opened the main and side doors of the coach and everybody departed.

Fortunately, it wasn't raining which would have made the mile long walk more of an annoyance than usual. Jack and I were making a good pace although I suspected Jack's pace was due to the fact that there was most likely a pub somewhere up ahead. I looked back momentarily as the elderly passengers of the coach walked slowly occasionally stopping and wheezing. No doubt this would be reported back to Pratt's coach firm before the day was over which wouldn't look good for Golden Trip Coaches. Eventually we got to the market square of the town which was bustling with various market stalls and people wanting to buy things as diverse as DVDs and tablecloths! Jack then noticed a pub called The Square Head and headed straight into it. I agreed to meet him in there later but first I needed some souvenirs.

I found several shops all in a row where fridge magnets, pens, pencils and other trinkets could be found. Within the first ten minutes of finding the shops I had already spent thirty quid including a lovely ceramic model of the market square which would take pride of place with all of my other models I had acquired on this holiday back at home. There didn't seem to be much else of note in Cowshit however and I spent the next hour wandering around perusing the market stalls and admiring a few Georgian buildings. I treated myself to a cup of cream tea and a scone in a local cafe and then sat on a bench in the market square for around half an hour before making my way to the pub I had seen Jack enter.

The Square Head was much like all of the other pubs around the area. It was nothing special but it did hold the same kind of friendly atmosphere one would expect from a village or town pub. I found Jack sitting next to a woman with a pint of lager in one hand and his other hand trying to get a purchase on the woman's right thigh without any luck due to the limb being heavily guarded by both of her hands! After the cream tea I couldn't stomach a full pint of bitter so I settled for just half which got me the accusation of being a wuss from Jack.

As soon as I sat at the same table as him and said, 'Hi,' the woman looked at me and smiled before shifting her position to sit next to me.

'Hi, handsome,' she said, 'my name's Laura — your creepy friend never told me he had such a nice-looking mate!'

'I'm not actually his mate,' I corrected her, 'I'm just a fellow coach traveller here on a day trip.'

'Still,' said the woman, 'you're still nice — you're a lot nicer than him.' She pointed at Jack as she said this.

'I'm afraid to tell you,' I said, 'that I already have a girlfriend. You're a nice enough woman but I'm not interested.'

'Shame,' said Laura looking disappointed, 'we could have had some good times together.'

Jack then moved so that he was sitting next to Laura which didn't go down too well with the woman.

'I'm single though babe,' he explained. 'How about we have a few good times together. What do you say?'

Laura seemed to be thinking of this offer for a few seconds — her face seemingly reflecting her being in deep thought. Eventually she gave Jack her answer.

'No thanks,' she answered before standing up and walking out of the pub.

'This is all your fault!' Jack then accused me.

'How is it my fault?' I asked.

'We were getting on well until you came in. She was just seconds away from begging me for sex until you came in and turned on the charm!'

'It didn't look that way from where I was standing,' I retorted. 'She was refusing all of your advances towards her.'

'Never!' replied the would-be Casanova. 'You see those

jeans she was wearing? All I needed was a few more seconds and she would be unzipping the fly and letting me in!'

'You live in such a fantasy world sometimes,' I replied, 'that it's incredible. One day I'll have to write a book about you so that everybody can laugh at your exploits!'

Jack stayed a little longer in the pub but I left after my half pint. The sun had come out and now the market square was awash with people enjoying the weather as well as buying things from the stalls. As I walked around I noticed a group of people entering the market square. I looked closer and it was all of the elderly people from the coach! They had only just made it into the hub of Cowshit and were clearly out of breath. Mr and Mrs Sneer were clearly disgruntled as were Mr and Mrs Stopwatch which didn't surprise me in the least. The Sneer family then noticed me and Mr Sneer waved his fist at me as to say, 'This is all your fault — you made the coach break down!' before all of the elderly descended on the café, I had enjoyed a cream tea in.

I spent the next hour just walking around Cowshit doing nothing special. The place was just another dull market town and as soon as I've seen and done everything I wanted to see and do the place lost its appeal. The elderly members of the coach holiday however found it fascinating as I noticed one couple walking into a shop and coming out with a bag full of shopping while another must have spent ages looking at a war memorial situated near the market stalls. Mr and Mrs Stopwatch spent all of their time in the cafe — no doubt complaining about the taste of the tea while Mr and Mrs Sneer were complaining about the prices of some of the items on the market stalls. I edged a little closer to catch what they were saying but could only catch the words '…this was a lot cheaper in my day. This is only worth threepence!' I didn't spot Everage and Norden but they were around somewhere — most likely admiring a thatched house or a cobbled pavement somewhere!

After I had got bored walking around the town I sat down on a wall staring at a block of public toilets for what seemed like hours! Is this what my daytrip had resorted to? Staring at some bogs because I'd already seen and done everything else! Finally, I walked to where the coach driver said he was going to pick us up and waited. Jack then joined me and eventually so too did the other elderly passengers. The coach wasn't here yet so Jack lit up a cigarette which caused Mr Sneer to shoot him a funny look.

'This will get the coach to turn up?' he then said to me as if his spat at the pub had now been forgotten.

'What will get the coach to turn up?' I asked him in reply.

'Having a fag,' he answered. 'If a bus doesn't turn up you can guarantee that it will as soon as you light up a fag!' The coach then arrived which put a smirk on Jack's face and parked close to where the driver said he would park. After the obligatory headcount once everybody had got on the coach the driver got going again and took a scenic route to Boggy Sands which should have only taken him about ten or fifteen minutes rather than the forty minutes it actually took. The driver announced that we were going to spend three hours here as opposed to the original plan of four hours due to the problems arising from the breakdown in Cowshit. I didn't need much time anyway. I only had plans to buy a few souvenirs and to have a look at the old Bunton's holiday area which would only take me about an hour or two anyway.

Boggy Sands was a place that I wouldn't enjoy a full

week's holiday at. At its peak it was an ideal holiday resort for parents with young kids and it still is to this day but not as much as it used to be. The seafront is now the hub of the small coastal town as opposed to the Bunton's resort a mile away which used to be packed during the summertime. After buying a few fridge magnets and a few obligatory pens and pencils I walked along the seafront with a small bag of chips en route to the Bunton's resort. When I finally reached the area it was all surrounded by wire fencing. A small sign on the fencing said in big red letters 'CONDEMNED' and underneath it 'DO NOT ENTER' while another sign read, 'coming soon: a new series of student apartment blocks and shopping centre'. So, this is what the Bunton's resort was going to be? The area was going to be redeveloped into something that didn't belong in a seaside resort. This made me angry. Suddenly images of the area in its heyday flooded into my memory. I had stayed here as a child for just one week and remembered the good times. When I revisited the place on a nostalgic trip recently I slipped underneath the wire fencing which could have been a bad idea because I was almost hit by the falling monorail train. The thought of which still sent shivers down my spine to this day.

I decided to take the risk once more and easily found the hole I had made in the wire fence the last time I was here and climbed through. I soon found the chalets which were looking more weathered than the last time. Another, 'CONDEMNED' sign was nailed to one of the walls of the chalets and some witty graffiti artist had written underneath, 'a new horror movie coming to a cinema near you soon!' More graffiti had been applied to the walls and many of the windows had been broken. One of the doors of the chalets was open and I chose to step inside. The chalet was devoid of all furniture as expected and more graffiti adorned the walls. I got fascinated with all the graffiti and spent the next five minutes reading some of them. As I was just about to leave I noticed another bit of graffiti which caught my attention.

'The KFC kid is in da house,' it read which rang a few bells. Where had I seen that graffiti before? At first I thought I must have read it the last time I was here but then it all came flooding back to me. It was written on the bus shelter near to where I lived as I was waiting for the feeder coach to take me to the service station at the beginning of the holiday! Whoever this 'KFC kid,' is he obviously goes to the same places as me! Finally I left the confines of the chalet and walked around the rest of the condemned resort.

I remembered where the swimming pools were and headed for them first. The Bunton's resort had one large swimming pool and several smaller ones and all of them were in a state of disrepair. I remembered swimming in the large pool as a child as my parents sat on loungers by the side of the pool but this was no longer possible. The large pool was empty and the edges were covered in graffiti and algae while all of the pool rides and ornaments such as slides and large plastic models of animals were lying on the floor of the empty pool — some of which hadn't been moved in years while others had been smashed by vandals. The smaller pools fared no better. One had been hastily filled in with concrete while another was almost full of rainwater and algae. A third was slightly filled with rainwater and a curious golden liquid. As I walked past these pools I noticed the derailed monorail nearby which had also been the victim of the graffiti artists and bad weather. I stooped down and pulled open one of the doors of the felled monorail train and looked inside. The seats were all still there and some were in good condition due to the exterior of the train taking all of the punishment from the bad weather, protecting everything inside.

As I explored the site further I discovered the radio room. This was where a chirpy-sounding woman spoke through a tannoy to all of the holidaymakers in the camp with news of competitions and prize giveaways. When I was very young I remember the woman informing us all of a swimming competition for the kids in which the prize was a day out at a local theme park (probably Fun Village Amusement Park). I remember competing but was soundly beaten by other, more better swimmers. The winner however was later disqualified because he subdued some of his competitors behind him by peeing in the pool as he swam!

The door of the radio room was locked but was hanging off its hinges. I grabbed the door and it swiftly came away in my hands. I entered the room and discovered that most of the radio equipment was missing but the basic tannoy system was still there. It was unplugged but maybe if the electricity hadn't been turned off on the site I could operate it. To my surprise the electricity was still working which made it even more dangerous to walk underneath the old monorail track because that could easily fall down and fry somebody! Whoever now owned this site obviously couldn't care less about safety and thought that a few wire fences was more than adequate. I picked up the microphone and plugged it in before sitting down on what was left of a chair after years of neglect had got to it. I then spoke into the microphone.

Good morning campers! Today we have a spot the spray can contest where the first person to find an empty spray can discarded by vandals will win a year's supply of spray cans!

We then have a pool filling contest where the first person to fill up one of the swimming pools with urine will win a free doctor's appointment to check why the hell you are passing so much water! Finally, we have a tour of the chalets where you can marvel at all of the swear words that have been written on the walls and also admire all of the chalet doors that have been busted down from constant kicking! Tonight's entertainment comes courtesy of somebody walking the entire length of the monorail line and getting toasted in the process!

After leaving the condemned site I walked back along the seafront which was a more pleasant and thriving area to look at. I grabbed another bag of chips and sat on the beach looking out to sea. I watched with some amusement as a bloke sped across the semi-hard sand wearing a pair of skis with a small jet pack of some description attached to each ski. As he moved at speed across the sand he whooped with joy scattering sunbathers and sandcastle building children in all directions! His joy came to a halt however when he came across someone with a bow and arrow doing archery practice. In normal circumstances I thought that somebody doing archery on a beach with kids was very dangerous but in this case I applauded him being there because, as soon as the jet-skier flew past him he redirected one of his arrows to one of the jet packs on one of the skis and fired. The small jet pack broke off and exploded while the remaining one propelled its rider into the sea and continued to drag him upside down until water put out the jet pack! The archer got a round of applause from all of the other beachgoers from this!

I treated myself to another bag of chips and also purchased more fridge magnets and sticks of rock before spending several minutes admiring the view out to sea. Jack then approached me with a larger bag of chips and a can of lager.

'So, what have you got up to?' he said as he washed down a handful of chips with a large gulp of lager.

'Nothing much,' I said, 'just been having a walk around the old Bunton's resort admiring the vandalism!'

Jack took another sip of lager and smiled. 'I've been watching bikini-clad girls frolicking on the beach!' he said, 'I'm also certain that that bird from the pub in Cowshit is here as well. I'm sure I saw her in a cracking bikini on the beach. Wonderful pair of legs she has as well!'

'Have been doing anything else other than being a pervert?' I asked him.

'Not really,' came the reply. 'I had to nip into a shop for this can of grog a few minutes ago but otherwise it's all been tough work staring at lovely women in tight bikinis!'

The coach arrived just over an hour later ironically just as Jack had lit up a cigarette and as I approached it so too did Mr and Mrs Sneer. As expected Mr Sneer waved his fist at me and Jack for reasons I never quite understood before boarding the coach which Jack thought it amusing to wave his fist back at him! The surprised look from Mr Sneer that followed was amusing as it was the first time during the holiday that I had seen him with anything other than an angry face! The other elderly guests all boarded the coach at a casual pace and then me and Jack boarded. The obligatory headcount was conducted by the driver and then the coach got moving.

On the journey back I looked out of the windows and read many of the road signs we passed. We had only been on the road for about two minutes when we passed a sign that said, 'Claptout-by-the-Sea 2 miles' which indicated that we would be back in our hotel in no time at all. This however was Golden

Trip Coaches and no doubt he would go on a magical mystery tour before we arrived back at the resort. A short while later I spotted a sign that read, 'Claptout-by-the-Sea 5 miles' and then a sign that read, 'Boggy Sands 2 miles'. Moments later a sign pointed out that we were only half a mile away from Boggy Sands despite spending the past fifteen minutes on the road. Another couple of minutes passed and we drove through Cowshit. This time the coach didn't break down and we were soon driving through Dogshit and then Bullshit before we passed Horseshit. After thirty-five minutes on the road we passed a sign that said, 'Claptout-by-the-Sea 2 miles' which I was certain was the same one we had passed a short while before. Finally, we got back into Claptout-by-the-Sea and I headed back up to the hotel room for a quick lie down on the broken bed that I had yet to report.

Chapter 13
A Mixed Night

Due to the chips I had eaten in Boggy Sands, I was only hungry enough for the slops that the hotel restaurant served up. Tracey had suggested we go out for a meal again but I declined so we instead decided on alternative amusement. The plan was this: I have dinner in the hotel restaurant and then Tracey meets me in the hotel reception a short while after. Together we would go into the hotel bar and have a couple of drinks, a game of bingo and watch the start of the hotel entertainment (which, according to the poster was a solo male singer who looked like a cross between Tom Jones, Buddy Holly and Elvis Presley). At first I thought that non guests wouldn't be allowed to have a drink in the bar but it turned out that they were allowed as long as they were accompanied by a guest of the hotel. Tracey seemed enthusiastic down the phone when I had called her after arriving back from Boggy Sands as she had never stayed in a hotel that was as poor as I had described before and she was looking forward to having a few chuckles at the expense of the cantankerous elderly hotel guests and the hotel entertainment.

As I had expected, Mr and Mrs Stopwatch were now seated at the same table as another elderly couple who had largely kept themselves to themselves during the holiday thus far. The unfortunate couple however soon found themselves on the receiving end of the Stopwatch family's attitude problem and were heavily chastised for talking to each other while the Stopwatch's were eating their meal. Mr Sneer was observing the drama unfold from his table nearby and seemed to side with the Stopwatch's as they insulted their new tablemates. The unfortunate couple then walked out of the restaurant after their meal feeling upset as Mr Sneer waved his fist at them and then Mr and Mrs Stopwatch performed their ritual of throwing their napkin down on the table in anger before walking out. I observed this from my original table with Jack and both found this amusing. Mr Sneer however didn't share my amusement as he suddenly faced me and waved his fist at me! Jack retorted by returning the gesture just as he had done at Boggy Sands which again, left Mr Sneer looking bemused!

After dinner I met Tracey in the reception and we hugged as if we hadn't seen each other in weeks before we both purchased bingo tickets and headed to the bar. I brought myself a beer and got Tracey a vodka and coke before sitting down on a table directly opposite Mr Sneer who clearly wasn't happy with the arrival of a non-guest in the hotel bar. Mr Sneer waved his fist at me which was now starting to become his signature greeting and I was considering going to the bookies the following morning to put a bet on how many times he would wave his fist at me or anybody else for that matter before the holiday was over!

'He's such a miserable old sod!' Tracey exclaimed.

'I know,' I replied, 'but it's all good fun!'

'Touch my breasts and my thighs and see how he reacts,' Tracey then whispered to me. I was taken aback by this as our relationship had never developed to this stage thus far. 'Go on — do it,' she whispered with a smile. I did so and Mr Sneer was surprised at first but then quickly became offended and he walked out of the bar with his wife in tow. Tracey giggled and I returned my hands to their normal positions and awaited round one of Cockney Rhyming Slang Bingo now with two less people playing the game!

Tracey won the house in the first game of bingo which seemed to offend Mr and Mrs Stopwatch and Norden won the second house. I won the third house which tipped Mr Stopwatch over the edge and he threw his bingo tickets down on the table and walked out of the bar feeling cheated!

'I'm enjoying tonight,' Tracey then giggled, 'I've never been so amused in my life!'

'You like offending people do you?' I asked.

'Yep,' Tracey said smiling, 'especially the ones who deserve to be offended!'

The hotel entertainment then came on and at first I thought he was one of the hotel guests until he came up on stage to sing. Wearing large Buddy Holly glasses and an Elvis Presley sparkly suit he looked like a librarian letting his hair down by going to a Saturday Night Fever type disco! I expected him to start singing anything by the King himself but he got into a routine of old crooner type songs. After a second drink had been duly finished off we decided to leave the bar and head out to find somewhere else to go. As we walked past reception I noticed Jack trying to chat up another new receptionist without any luck. The dusk in Claptout-by-the-Sea was starting to set and the evening seemed beautiful. Tracey commented on how amazing the sky looked and I had to agree with her. As we took a slow walk down the road we took time to admire several old buildings and hotels.

Our first stop was a small bar attached to a nearby hotel

and as we sat in a couple of outdoor chairs on an overhanging balcony we again gazed at the sky as it turned from light red to dark red and then a dark blue / black colour. I found it amazing that if I had been sitting here on my own I most likely would have ridiculed this kind of evening but Tracey made me feel different about it. The idyllic romantic scenario was however punctuated by a few glimpses of things that deserved ridicule. A nearby pub had the unfortunate task of evicting a drunk patron and the landlord did the cartoon-style of eviction of throwing somebody out by the collar of his shirt in one hand and the waist of his trousers in the other! Once out the drunk bumped into a lamppost and apologised to it in his drunken tone of voice before walking elsewhere in a zig-zag pattern.

We only had a couple of drinks in this bar before moving on. Whenever I was on holiday I normally tended to stick to the first good bar I found throughout the holiday but Tracey introduced me to the notion of staying only a short while in one bar before moving onto another one.

'You don't know which are the good bars until you try them,' she pointed out, which I had to agree with. We tried another hotel bar with a less scenic view for just one drink each before trying out a pub a few doors down from the Punk Establishment. This one was your typical village pub with sticky carpets and we drunk up quickly (which probably wasn't the best idea if we were going to go to other places and try to remain as sober as possible) before leaving. The next one we tried was the bar owned by the bloke who I had referred to as Steptoe earlier on. There was live music on and, like the Claptout Hotel it only did the old stuff. Tracey appeared to enjoy the music more than me and she got more and more romantic towards me as the night went on although that was perhaps more to do with the amount of drink she had had rather than the entertainment. We seemed to have spent a lot longer in here than in the other bars and by the end we were nearly half drunk (I was most likely more than half drunk but I felt less than half drunk). In the end Steptoe gave us a cursory eye as we left and his original refusal to not let Tracey play at his bar now seemed justified.

We made the slow walk back to the hotel after this and subsequently crashed down in a couple of seats in the hotel bar. The bar was no longer serving drinks but the barman was happy to serve us a glass of water each. Other than the barman we were the only ones left in the room and the lights had dipped as music from a CD played through some speakers at low volume while we kissed almost non-stop. The singer had long since packed up and gone home and all of the other hotel guests had retreated to bed while we remained down in the bar. Eventually however, we conceded the night was over and we left the bar. Tracey left the hotel and back to her car which worried me because she wasn't really in the right state of mind to drive while I retreated to my hotel room. I had however only navigated one set of stairs before I collapsed out and fell asleep!

Chapter 14
Mixing with the Scruffs

I woke up the next morning with mixed feelings. This was my last full day at Claptout-by-the-Sea and I was going to miss the place when I left. What had started out as an average but moderately enjoyable holiday had quickly turned into a wonderful holiday where I had met people I would not forget in a long time.

I had forgotten to draw the curtains in my hotel room the previous night so the early morning light shone through the holes in the net curtains casting a series of dots on the far wall of my room. I remember falling asleep on the stairs the previous night but how I made it back into my room I didn't know! Perhaps I had woken up an hour or so later and finally completed the rest of the journey up to my room. I looked at the time on my mobile phone which was lying upside down on the bedside cabinet and slumped back down on the bed causing it to collapse! It was only six o'clock in the morning but already I was wide awake. I got dressed and walked out of my room and down into reception where the young lady who Jack tried to chat up a couple of days previously was on duty. The young girl smiled at me and I walked out of the hotel to catch some of the early morning air.

Jack was outside with his now obligatory cigarette in his mouth.

'You must have had a cracking night last night,' he

commented as he saw me.

'I did,' I replied. 'I got a little bit wrecked!'

Jack laughed as I said this. 'I know,' he said back, 'I came down to the reception to have another crack at that bird on reception and I found you asleep on the stairs! After finding out what room you were in I contacted the manager and got him to take you up to your room.'

'Thanks,' I said gratefully, 'I appreciate it.'

'I didn't do it for you,' Jack then said, 'I thought that maybe if I helped a friend in need then the sexy babe on reception would see me as some kind of caring sort and fall for me!'

'And did she?' I said, my gratefulness for him depleted.

'Did she hell,' spat Jack, 'she just looked at me and carried on filing her nails!'

Jack soon put out his cigarette and walked back inside while I chose to go for an early morning walk. Suddenly I saw Tracey's car parked nearby. I walked over to it and noticed that Tracey was asleep inside at the wheel still wearing last night's clothing. The driver's door was unlocked so I opened it and gently shook her on the shoulder to wake her. She awoke looking groggy and yawned before looking at me.

'What the hell happened last night?' she asked as she gripped her forehead with both hands.

'We had too much pop,' I said.

'Seriously?' she replied. 'If that's the case then I've lived up to my band name!' I helped Tracey out of her car and suggested we take a short walk. Tracey agreed and locked up her car before embarking on the walk — our arms wrapped around each other seemingly in a loving posture but really it was just to keep us both from falling over!

We took the short walk along the seafront and along the beach looking at all of the other hotels and cafe's surrounding the area as we let our hangovers slowly leave our bodies. Golden Trip Holidays must have chosen the worst hotel in the area because others looked far nicer and even had names such as Hotel Exquisite and Hotel Paris. I looked up at some of these nicer looking, more modern hotels and wondered what they were like inside. Maybe one day me and Tracey would book a holiday here together and stay in one of these hotels. Judging by the exterior I guessed these hotels were posh on the inside and had large spacious restaurants with wonderful tasting food and large hotel rooms commanding excellent views of the beach. Of course, I could be wrong and they were probably no better than my own hotel on the inside with views of somebody's backyard!

We walked into a cafe that opened early every morning and sat down as I ordered a coffee each. Throughout the holiday I had walked past this cafe without giving it any thought but this morning I decided to give it a try. As we drunk the coffee I got into a conversation with the owner of the shop where I found out a few things about Claptout-by-the-Sea and its residents — most of which weren't exactly fascinating but still insightful. The owner — a middle-aged woman of about fifty informed me that the man who used a catapult to dispose of his dog's waste, was a certain Mr Johnson who had been doing the same thing for years. He was even once arrested when he catapulted the waste into the sea during a junior swimming tournament and the waste hit a young girl in the face! The two warring radio-controlled aircraft operators were none other than Jack Stone and Barry Wilkinson who had been warring for years and were now so well known for their spats that people tended to stay well away from them when they flew their RC aircraft so that the crashed wreckage wouldn't fall on their heads! The waxwork museum used to be owned by a man who thought he was a fantastic celebrity caricaturist and all of his waxworks were designed on his own personal sketches rather than actual photos. It is rumoured that when he died his spirit resided in one of the more grotesque waxworks and frightened some visitors in the few years following his death! The new owner still makes current waxworks from badly drawn sketches because it is rumoured that he once introduced a waxwork that looked exactly like who it was supposed to be but it bizarrely burst into flames one night and almost set the building on fire! The new owner considered this a message from the previous owner to only use bad caricatures of celebrities and has done so ever since!

As we finished our coffee, the shop owner asked what plans we had for today. I explained that I was going on a coach trip to Scruff today which caused the woman to tut loudly.

'What a horrible place,' she opined. 'Full of kids pretending they're the bees' knees!'

'I've been there once before when I was younger,' I said 'but I *was* younger then and people mistook me for one of them. Now that I'm a bit older I expect to be treated differently.'

'Oh, you will,' said the owner, 'the Scruffs over there hate anybody who looks over the age of thirty. They seem to treat everybody who's not one of them terribly.' I then thought about how Mr Sneer would react in the city. I had a feeling that his fist-waving antics would go into overdrive today. He appeared to hate everybody who was younger than him and the amount of times he waved his fist would surely be a new world record! We then bade farewell to the coffee shop owner and carried onwards further along the road.

We reached Rusty Pier and witnessed Mr Johnson clean up after his dog in his own unique way before carrying onwards. Suddenly I remembered that we had promised to visit the Claptout-by-the-Sea's dungeon attraction at some point.

'I think it's too late for that now,' smiled Tracey still feeling a little bit tipsy but nowhere near as bad as when I had found her in her car a little earlier.

'It's always the same whenever I go on holiday,' I reminisced, 'I always make plans to do things but then forget them and only remember to do them when it's too late!'

'You're not the only one,' replied Tracey, 'I've missed band practice before and didn't realise until one of the band phoned me up!'

'Have you got any band practice today?' I then asked to which Tracey shook her head. We walked a little further before choosing to walk back to the hotel. While I had breakfast, Tracey decided that she would just sit in the hotel bar with a soft drink before driving off to Scruff to meet me as I came off the coach there. I did question if she was okay to drive and she explained that she was. I still wasn't totally convinced but she was adamant she was fine. Besides, she was looking forward to visiting Scruff. Tracey admitted that she had never been to Scruff before because she considered all of the college and university students to be nothing more than educated zombies! From what she had heard and also what she had seen on news clips on the TV the students who plagued Scruff walked around in packs seemingly hunting for fresh meat — or in this case non-students. Anybody who wasn't a student at one of the many colleges and universities in Scruff was considered the enemy. It was the equivalent of walking into the proverbial lion's den. Tracey might actually be able to get away with looking like a Scruff because she was still young-looking and beautiful enough to be mistaken for one but I might be considered to be a 'granddad' around town. How all of the elderly hotel residents would look is anyone's guess but it would be fun to find out! I expected them all to be hit with insults from all sides from the students which would certainly put the wind up Mr Stopwatch and Mr Sneer!

After fighting through the breakfast queue I returned to my room and sat down for a moment with another cup of coffee. I observed from my window some woman taking a black bin bag of rubbish out and putting it in the dustbin before walking back indoors. Moments later a man walked out and chose to go looking through the rubbish inside the bin before retrieving a pair of drumsticks! The woman then came back outside and, although I never heard what she was saying I guessed she was arguing with the man. I could be wrong but I assumed that the woman had thrown the drumsticks away to try and stop the man from playing the drums. The man then walked back indoors followed shortly afterwards by the woman.

I walked into the restaurant about ten or fifteen minutes later and discovered that the game of musical chairs was still in full swing. Mr and Mrs Stopwatch were still on their latest table in the restaurant but the original elderly couple were now sitting at the Stopwatch's old table by the window! I actually felt sorry for this couple because their holiday had been partly ruined by a couple of miserable old people who seemingly were hell bent on bringing down the hotel and possibly even the coach company. As I ate my English breakfast I asked Jack if he was looking forward to visiting Scruff.

'Of course, I am,' he remarked. 'There are a shitload of student bars over there and I'll be sampling the beer in several of them!'

'So, you're not interested in the sightseeing then?' I asked.

'I'll be doing a lot of sightseeing,' he replied, 'it's the time of year when all of the female students come out in miniskirts and there's no way I'll be missing these views!'

Somehow I expected Jack to come out with an answer like that!

The coach pulled up outside the hotel at nine o'clock and as the elderly members of the coach boarded I stood by the side of Tracey's car speaking to her. In the half hour or so that I had been 'enjoying' breakfast she had driven back home and had a shower and a change of clothes. She was also a bit more sober which prompted me to believe that she had also had another cup of coffee. When I was sure that I could reach my seat on the coach without having to stand behind a queue of slow moving passengers I kissed Tracey farewell for the moment and boarded the coach. Tracey then drove off en route to Scruff where she would meet up with me again although how long she would have to wait for the coach to arrive was anybody's guess!

As the coach pulled off the driver spoke through the intercom.

'We will soon be arriving in Scruff,' he said which could be roughly translated as, 'we will be arriving in Scruff in about five hours' time after we have driven through a dozen different villages of no great importance!'

'Scruff is a college and university city and many of the

residents there are students. All of them are studying for various degrees and qualifications but can still find time to enjoy themselves.' As a former student of a smaller college I had a good idea how students 'enjoyed themselves' and it all depended on whether they had a sex-mad girlfriend or they were a sexually frustrated single guy! My college days incorporated the latter of these but I held out hope that one day I would fall into the former category! Hopefully I wouldn't accidently witness these students 'enjoying themselves' while I was there today!

The coach driver then went on about the arrangements for tomorrow.

'Because tomorrow is your final day here in Claptout-by-the-Sea the hotel has requested that you all leave your cases outside your hotel room before 8am tomorrow morning so that the porters can bring them all down and load them back onto the coach. The hotel has also requested that you all hand in your keys to your rooms shortly after breakfast as we will be departing at around half past nine.' This message brought a lump to my throat. It was a signal that the holiday was almost over — a holiday which I had enjoyed for various reasons. After coming back from Scruff later on I had to pay a visit to some of the amusements again for two reasons. The first was to trade in all of the tickets I had won from the slot machines over the course of the week and the second was to enjoy myself in the resort one last time — maybe even visit the dungeon I had promised myself or even have a game of bingo in the local casino that I had also promised myself but had forgotten as soon as Tracey came into my life. Claptout-by-the-Sea had dragged me into all of its attractions to such a degree I wanted to return here again next year.

It was a full hour before we reached Scruff even though it was only about half an hour down the road. The coach driver told us that we were going to be picked up again at 5pm before we all departed and the coach drove off to a nearby coach park. He had left us in the city centre surrounded by the biggest collection of Scruffs I'd ever seen. As soon as some of them saw the elderly members of the coach party the insults started to fly. Mr Sneer walked past one small group of Scruffs and wasted no time in waving his fist at each individual member! This was a bad decision as they retaliated instantly.

'Go on, hop it, you old coot,' said one.

'Go back to your Zimmer frame and get lost,' said another.

'Piss off and take your mobility scooter with you, you old fart!' retorted a third. This caused Mr Sneer to put on his surprised face once more which made me snigger!

I watched Jack disappear into a student bar called The Bar Stud before I phoned Tracey.

'Where are you?' I asked.

'I'm outside the Tudor campus of Scruff University East,' she replied.

'I'm not all that far away from you,' I said, 'I'm outside the Victorian campus of the same university. Wait there I'll meet you.'

Scruff University East had several campuses all named after various royal families over the centuries and I had to pass the Norman Campus and the Stuart Campus before reaching the Victorian Campus (which should have been called the Hanover Campus because Queen Victoria was a member of that family and not some family who had a surname that matched her first name — I knew my history!) I walked the short distance to where Tracey was and in no time I had found

147

her despite the area teeming with students. I was just about to hold her hand when a young male student came up to me and challenged me for her. This was standard procedure at some colleges. If one male liked the look of an already taken for female he would challenge the boyfriend for her hand. I remember foolishly doing it once with a kid who was a couple of years older than me and was a rugby pro. His girlfriend was a cheerleader and therefore had to be beautiful and have a perfect figure. Needless to say I lost but what was even more annoying was that when I came out of hospital a few days later I discovered that he had split with her and was now going out with somebody else! I could have waited a day or two and I would probably have had a serious chance.

This young Scruff was a little shorter than me and also about ten years younger. He obviously thought he could beat me solely on account of our ages because, like me when I was his age, he thought that everybody over the age of thirty was physically weak and unable to defend against even the merest slap across the face!

'So you think you can beat me fair and square?' I said as Tracey hung off my shoulder like some devoted girlfriend half wanting me to just walk away but also half wanting me to rough him up a little.

'Piece of piss!' He exclaimed! (Terms such as 'piece of piss' always made me ponder the realism of the phrase. Piss is a liquid and not a solid so therefore how can you possibly have a piece of piss unless it is frozen and even if it is frozen you have to seriously question why urine is frozen in the first place — especially if there isn't any cold weather around!)

The match was over in no time as I gave him a small jab in the stomach and slapped him across the face — I was never one for violence which made me ponder what moves I would have done on the rugby pro all those years ago! The young Scruff then went running away almost in tears and me and Tracey continued our walk through the city of Scruffs.

After this little altercation me and Tracey had a slow walk around the city passing a few student protesters as we did so. One group protested against the allocation of fresh air for people who didn't share the same opinion as them while another protested against the university's grass being longer than a few inches! Another group wasn't quite a group of protesters but rather a campaign organisation. As far as I could work out they wanted the Lady Jane Grey Campus rebuilt after it had followed in the way of its namesake and disappeared after just nine days! To be fair the Lady Jane Grey Campus was nothing more than a series of large tents and a strong gust of wind a few days ago had laid waste to the temporary campus. This group wanted it reinstated as a series of tents again but the university's organisers were against the idea. The students were furious and campaigned to try and change the organisers' minds.

After leaving this university behind, Tracey and I admired our surroundings.

'Don't you think that city breaks are romantic?' Tracey said.

'Yes, I do,' I replied, 'but I've never really enjoyed a city break with a woman before so I couldn't really experience the romantic side of it.'

'Your mate obviously sees some kind of romantic interest in the city,' Tracey then said as she pointed just ahead of us. About ten metres in front was Jack who had his arms draped around the shoulders of two college girls and talking like some kind of charmer to them.

'What do you think he sees in those two,' said Tracey, 'they look a bit too young for him. They must be about ten years younger than him!'

'Look at what they're wearing and you'll find your answer!' I replied.

The two girls, who only looked in their early twenties were both wearing short skirts exposing a pair of shapely legs each. Every few seconds I noticed Jack's head drop in between short bursts of his various chat-up lines. It was obvious he was more interested in what was below the waistline than what these women had inside their heads! We continued to walk slowly and decided to eavesdrop on what Jack was saying to the two Scruffs.

'So ladies, what are you two beauties doing tonight?'

The two girls looked at each other before giving their answer.

'I'm washing my hair,' said one, 'but maybe I could put it off for one night.'

'I'm studying for a course tomorrow,' said the other, 'but studying is boring and I could be tempted to put it on hold for a night.'

'How would you two beauties like a night on the town with me tonight — I can show you a real good time!'

The two young ladies seemed to be coming round to liking him. However, he soon ruined any chances he had given himself.

'Both of you two lovelies have a cracking set of legs each — how about we go to a nice bar and have a few drinks as you two come in the shortest skirts you have. Afterwards we could head to some nice quiet place where I could get to know your legs a lot better! What do you say?'

The two females then removed his arms from their shoulders and walked off! As they did so Jack gave them a nasty look before retorting 'pissing lesbians!' Me and Tracey decided not to console Jack over the failure of his latest conquest because he would no doubt blame us for it like he did with me in the pub in Cowshit. Instead we ducked into a nearby gift shop as he went in search of more women.

Me and Tracey spent about ten or so minutes in the gift shop. We had only intended to use the shop as a hideout so that Jack wouldn't see us but we ended up buying a few gifts. I purchased my obligatory clutch of fridge magnets, pens, pencils and also a posh-looking but ultimately cheap piece of jewellery for Tracey. Tracey herself brought several other pieces of cheap jewellery which made me feel a little better about me buying her cheap trinkets. When we left the gift shop, we noticed Jack in the near distance walking into another student bar — no doubt for the two 'B's' — beer and babes!

Over the course of the next two hours we visited more gift shops and brought more stuff that would clog up my fridge door back home as well as a lovely model of Scruff University East before we popped into a student bar for a quick drink. There we talked about the rest of our day.

'Do you fancy going for another curry in that Josh Rogan place again instead of dinner at the hotel?' Tracey suggested.

'Why not?' I replied, 'it'll be my last day in the holiday resort so might as well make the most of it.'

'Good,' Tracey smiled. 'The Six Pissed Dolls have also got a gig tonight as well at the Punk Establishment again — so how about staying there for our final night here?'

'I'd love it. The last time I went there to see the band we

didn't know each other so it would be a nice change. Jack might also be there though. No doubt he'll be looking up your skirt again!'

'So what?' Tracey giggled. 'Let him look at my knickers! At least you'll know that sometime you'll be getting inside them but he won't!'

'You have such an interesting sense of humour,' I said finally 'every woman I've been with before has been coy about such subjects but you are different. You don't mind joking about certain subjects of womanhood.'

'As I've said before,' Tracey explained, 'I'm a punk chick — I do things differently to other girls!'

I couldn't complain about that explanation.

We had a couple of drinks in the student bar before we left just as Jack was entering. Whether he saw us or not, we don't know but he didn't acknowledge it if he did. We then passed Mr and Mrs Sneer upsetting more Scruffs as if he hadn't learned his lesson last time. This time Mr Sneers fist waving was answered by a Scruff who spat at him! We laughed quietly by ourselves and walked past to discover Everage and Norden being insulted by more Scruffs. The elderly couple however didn't seem to pay a bit of notice and just walked onwards which is what Mr Sneer should have done. Finally, we discovered Mr and Mrs Stopwatch talking to their son who was sitting on the steps of his coach. We tried to catch what they were talking about as their conversations were always amusing but when we got near Mr Stopwatch noticed us and suddenly stopped talking. He obviously didn't want us hearing what he was saying. As soon as we were out of earshot, he continued to talk again — which no doubt including some negative gossip about me and Tracey!

The coach arrived a couple of hours later by which time most of its passengers had had enough of Scruff. 'Bloody vandals,' exclaimed Mr Sneer as he stepped onto the coach which was echoed by Mr Stopwatch although his opinion included one or two cuss words that were quite tame in comparison to today's swear words but were no doubt frowned upon in his younger days. I kissed Tracey farewell and then she drove off as I got onto the coach. The driver had seemingly had another conversation with a fellow driver as he explained once more that somebody had questioned why he took the scenic route instead of the direct route. Like the last time he 'proved' that his way was the quickest by going the same route back to Claptout-by-the-Sea as suggested by the other coach driver. Also, like last time we were back in the holiday resort within ten minutes!

I returned to my hotel room and freshened up by showering and slipping into a nice shirt and trousers. I was starting to run out of clean clothing but that was how I always planned my holidays. On the final full day of the holidays I always found myself with either no clean clothes or only one decent set of clean clothes. The worst occasion in memory was when I went on holiday a few years ago and I was caught out in the pouring rain on no less than three occasions and even went on a log flume at a nearby amusement park which also soaked my clothes! By the final day I was wearing the same clothes I had worn on the first day which had been wet but had subsequently dried on the hotel room radiator overnight!

I met Tracey again in the hotel reception who had also changed into a nice knee-length red dress. We got into her car and headed once more to the Josh Rogan restaurant we had eaten in the other evening and there we bumped into George

Brewer once more. He asked Tracey if she had got anything sorted with her solo career yet but she just shook her head. I then interrupted to save face.

'We're both working on it,' I said, 'it's not easy you see. Tracey has got band practice most days and is even performing at the Punk Establishment tonight so she can only sort things out in between gigs and practice.'

'I understand,' said George, 'it's a bugger when you want to start something new but other things get in your way. I've known several bands over the years who have been like that. I'll have to nip down to the Establishment tonight to see you. I haven't seen the band for a few months and I enjoyed your music last time.'

George left the restaurant a short while later and when he did Tracey looked at me with a fiendish look in her eyes.

'I think I might wear my shortest skirt tonight for the gig,' she said to my surprise, 'and I'll try and convince the other girls to do the same. I want to see the look on your mate's face when he sees us!'

'Will the venue let you wear such things?' I asked.

'Of course,' smiled Tracey. 'I once saw a gig there where the female lead singer left little to the imagination. I've seen nudists with more clothing on!'

'I would have liked to have seen that,' I commented.

'I bet you would!' said Tracey with a laugh, 'and I bet your mate would have tried to get a bit closer to the performer if he was there!'

'He'd probably ask her to donate one of her items of clothing to him "for charity" knowing him!'

'His "charity" would most likely be his wedding tackle!' giggled Tracey.

After we had finished eating we walked to Tracey's car and got in. As we drove to my hotel I asked her what time her gig would finish.

'Do you hate it that much you want it to be over quickly?' she asked half seriously.

'Of course not,' I replied. 'I was only saying because the hotel entertainment is usually reasonably good on the final night of the holiday. I was thinking maybe we could catch up with it after the gig.'

'If it's anything like the one last night it would be bloody hilarious!' Tracey then exclaimed.

'So, what do you say?' I asked finally.

'If we finish in a good enough time we'll get away as soon as we've packed everything away and go back to the hotel to see whatever silly routine is being played out tonight!'

Chapter15
The Final Night

I got back to my hotel room just as Jack was exiting his. The self-proclaimed lothario was all dressed up in a smart shirt and trousers and smelled vaguely of some expensive aftershave. I didn't need to ask him where he was going because I had a very good idea.

'Going for a good night out,' I asked him as I passed by.

'Of course,' he replied with a smile as he ran his hands down his shirt as if to iron out any creases. 'I'm going to see the Six Pissed Dolls at the Punk Establishment tonight — which I'm sure you're already aware of.

'I am, yes,' I replied hoping that the band would wear outfits that would come close to giving Jack a heart attack!

'You've most likely already had one of the members up against a wall until she's singing the details of the gig out to you! In fact, I'd go as far as say that you've banged the lot of them in one great big orgy!'

'You should write a book,' I replied sarcastically, 'one of those badly written erotic novels for women with a title that sounds like a DIY shop colour chart but with only one colour available.'

'That sounds like a good idea,' said Jack, with a hint of sarcasm to match my own. 'Of course I would have to be the leading guy who gets all the women.'

'Might be a good seller but it would have to have a

disclaimer notice pointing out that it's nothing but pure fiction!'

'Ha bloody ha!' was Jack's dry response. He then 'ironed' shirt with his hands once more and started to move. 'Anyway, I'll see you at the Establishment. Bye!'

'Don't choke on your lager though,' I then said, 'and make sure you hold tightly onto your seat — I wouldn't want you to fall off and hurt yourself when you see the main attraction!'

'What do you mean by that,' replied Jack, as he stopped suddenly in his tracks.

'I just know one or two other things about the gig tonight. I'll say no more'

'Such as what?'

'That would be telling,' I smiled as I walked into my hotel room leaving Jack puzzled.

I got changed into a lovely shirt and trousers similar to that of Jack's attire but not identical as people might think we're twin brothers before walking to the venue. As I entered I walked towards the bar as I had arranged with Tracey and ordered myself a beer and took a seat near the front of the stage. I met Tracey prior to her coming on stage and she was wearing an almost obscenely short white dress which got Jack's attention immediately. He shuffled up to where I was sitting and whispered in my ear. 'Is this what you meant by you knowing "one or two things"?'

I nodded as I took a sip of my beer and put my arm around Tracey. Tracey then stood up and walked backstage as I observed Jack watching her leave (or rather, watching her thighs leave!).

The other band members then came on to the stage in similarly short dresses which caused great pain to Jack's eyesight as he didn't know where to look! His dumbfounded face was priceless to look at and he stared open-mouthed as a few other fans showed their admiration with wolf whistles. I was wondering if he would have vision problems before the end of the gig as looking at all of these legs and the obviously exposed underwear that resided at the tops of them wouldn't do him any favours!

The gig lasted just over an hour and during the gig I appreciated punk music more than I had ever done while Jack appeared to appreciate the female figure more than he had ever done if the smile on his face was anything to go by! I helped Tracey and the other band members pack away their gear and, to my surprise, so too did Jack. It was only afterwards on our walk back to the hotel that I suspected he only offered to help out because he still wanted to see more of the band from the waist down! After the band had packed up Tracey quickly slipped into a pair of jeans and a T-shirt backstage which disappointed Jack but made me feel a little easier as who knew what would happen in the hotel if the elderly residents saw a young woman wearing a dress that was so short it was almost touching her nose! Mr Sneer would most likely consider it pornography while I imagined that Mr Stopwatch would complain about how, in his day, he would be accused of being a pervert if he ogled a young woman's ankle!

We arrived at the hotel arm-in-arm and went into the hotel bar where the evening's entertainment had already begun. According to the poster in reception the bloke in question was a singer who had a wide repertoire of songs he could sing (which was most likely a lie) and could do random requests (which would be entertaining if the other residents of the hotel requested something that was even vaguely worth listening to!) His name was Cliff Thornton who I was sure used to be a famous snooker player but what do I know — I only ever watch darts on TV!

Me and Tracey got our first drink and watched as the singer, who was dressed like a cross between Timmy Mallett and Alan Sugar went around the room asking for requests. He never selected any songs of his choice but he did seem to sing quite a few 'old crooner' songs as chosen by people such as Mr and Mrs Stopwatch! Eventually Cliff came to us and he asked Tracey for a request. She selected a pop song from the late 1980's which I couldn't work out whether she was trying to annoy the elderly residents or to please me because I had a slight interest in music of that decade. She then revealed to the singer that she was a singer herself which prompted Cliff to invite her up on stage with him to tell him a little about herself. It turned out that he had seen one or two gigs from her now illustrious band and was delighted to share a stage with someone of such musical calibre! After he had performed her request he invited her to do a duet with him and he chose the song Something's Gotten Hold of my Heart which seemed to delight the elderly guests but also delighted me to a certain extent as the song was a big hit in my favourite decade of music. Cliff and Tracey did a wonderful rendition which even made Mr Sneer smile although the performance looked like a tribute act for the hosts of an old music show called The Hitman and Her! Cliff Thornton wasn't exactly young looking while Tracey looked old enough to be his daughter and the performance, although sounding great, was a bit uneasy looking if you happened to watch it!

After asking for more requests from the other guests Cliff and Tracey did another duet of a song which I wasn't familiar with but both of them were (it must have been a 1970's song because it sounded like one although I couldn't work out what the song was about. All I could work out was that the song was talking about a derriere made of stone because they were singing about a rock bottom at various points!) In fact, virtually all of the elderly guests were familiar with it which left me feeling a little left out. Tracey returned to her seat after this song and I brought her another drink as a kind of reward for making the hotel entertainment more interesting for the first time.

At the end of the night a few of the elderly residents thanked Tracey for the songs and even congratulated me on picking such a nice and polite young woman! Not that we were listening too much to them anyway because the combined alcohol consumption from three venues made us feel a little tipsy. Fortunately, Tracey wasn't quite inebriated enough to go for a spot of drink driving but I still wasn't happy about her getting behind the wheel anyway. She immediately agreed and phoned up one her band members who actually lived in Claptout-by-the-Sea who let her stay at her flat for the night. I walked her to her bandmates house before kissing her goodnight and then I walked slightly light-headed back to the hotel.

Chapter 16
Adventures in a Garden Centre

Today was the very last day I would be in Claptout-by-the-Sea — at least for the moment anyway. As I sorted out the collapsed bed for the final time I thought about the holiday and what joys it had brought me. I had experienced good times such as meeting Tracey and bad times such as getting caught in the rain and being terrified as I rode on the Ferris wheel. I had also experienced amusing moments from the locals on the beach and the elderly residents in the hotel. No holiday was ever a bad one because you always took back fond memories of it. The constant sight of a man catapulting his pets' excrement into the sea wasn't exactly something I wanted to remember but it would be stuck with me now — it was something that I found amusing to a certain degree which was what made it memorable.

It was just past seven o'clock in the morning and there was much shuffling outside my hotel room door. Everybody else was up and were placing their cases outside of their rooms ready for the hotel porters to take them downstairs so that the coach driver could load them back onto the coach. I fitted all of my clothing and several of my trinkets into the case and dropped it outside my hotel room door before retreating back inside to pack as much into my hand luggage bag as I could. When I arrived at Claptout-by-the-Sea my hand luggage bag was almost empty but now it weighed a ton! This was normal for me whenever I went on holiday as I always tended to come back with far too much stuff. A couple of years ago I went on holiday and came back with my hand luggage weighing almost as much as my main case and also about five plastic carrier bags full of souvenirs as well! This then made me think. Earlier on in the holiday I remembered one elderly couple pop into a supermarket and come back out with what appeared to be their weekly shopping. I laughed at this at the time and to a certain extent I still am now because I can't think of one single good reason why anybody would want to go on holiday and do their family shopping! That said however they most likely have less plastic bags to carry back than me as I now had four bags full of various trinkets to clutter my house with back home.

As I drunk a cup of bog-standard hotel room coffee I decided to give Tracey a call to see how she was. Her friend answered the phone.

'Hi,' I said, 'is Tracey awake yet?'

'Yes, she is — but only just! You sure are an early riser — you're just like your friend Jack.'

'You know Jack?' I asked puzzled.

'Of course, I do,' she said, 'I'm Jenny from the Six Pissed Dolls and after you and Tracey deserted us last night me and Jack stayed behind and had a few drinks and found we had a lot in common.'

I was starting to understand where all of this was leading but I assumed that there was only one thing the pair had in common. Jack liked a great pair of legs and Jenny no doubt possessed them!

'Jack stayed here with me last night but he's already left to sort out his luggage. He's quite a demon in the bedroom!'

'That's a bit too much information!' I said back but then

realised that he had conquered one of the Six Pissed Dolls whereas I hadn't yet! It wasn't a big deal however. Me and Tracey were more into slow, developing relationships whereas Jack — and no doubt Jenny were into fast love! Jenny then passed the phone onto Tracey and the conversation continued.

'Can you believe that Jenny slept with your mate last night!' she said in a surprised tone of voice.

'I can actually,' I replied, 'I've only known Jack for a few days and already I feel like I've known him for years. He strikes me as one of those sex-on-a-first-date kind of people and I'm guessing Jenny is too.'

'Only when she's had a few drinks,' replied Tracey., 'It was Jenny who came up with the name the Six Pissed Dolls after we had been out all-night drinking once and we came back a little bit ill. Jenny always has sex on a first date if a bloke buys her a lot of drinks!'

'Maybe I should have dated her then,' I joked.

'Do you like women like that?' she then asked me.

'Not really,' I said, 'I was only joking.'

'Good,' said Tracey, 'because you won't get any sex out of me for at least six months!'

I went down to breakfast soon after I had put the phone down and was surprised to find Jack already in the restaurant. Throughout the entire holiday I had always beat him into the restaurant for breakfast but here he was ahead of me today! I didn't need to ask him why he was here before me because I had a suspicion he was still on a high after last night. Nevertheless, I chose to pretend I wasn't aware of the situation.

'That receptionist is on duty again this morning,' I said to Jack as he tucked into a full English breakfast.

'So what,' he replied between mouthfuls. 'I don't go for those kind of girls — I'm more into the kind of punk chick. I like girls who like the same kind of music as me.'

'You mean like a member of the Six Pissed Dolls?' I said which got a few funny looks from the other elderly guests as soon as I uttered the 'P' word.

'You know more than you're letting on aren't you,' he then said, 'Tracey has told you about last night, hasn't she?'

'Yes, she has,' I nodded as my breakfast arrived.

Once I had made it clear that I knew about his final night in Clapout-by-the-Sea, Jack couldn't stop talking about his conquest throughout breakfast which would have been okay if the rest of the restaurant wasn't filled with elderly people. Many times he mentioned the band name and other times he explained in detail what went on between him and Jenny last night. Unsurprisingly Mr Sneer wasn't best pleased and gave us both a funny look. Obviously his delight at Tracey's singing last night had been left in the hotel room and his normal demeanour had returned. Mr and Mrs Stopwatch walked out of the restaurant in their usual fashion while Everage and Norden seemed not to be bothered in the slightest as they carried on with their breakfast without a single word or negative comment uttered. I was beginning to wonder if this pair even had the ability to talk!

When breakfast had finished, Jack and I returned to our respective hotel rooms and packed away any last things we had left out in the room before going back down to reception. I watched as one of the hotel porters packed everybody's cases onto the waiting coach with sadness. This marked the official end of the holiday. As soon as all of the cases were loaded it would be time to board the coach. The reception area was starting to fill up with all of the other guests who were departing as I stood there as well as a lot of new holidaymakers just starting their vacation entering the hotel. I pushed through the crowd and handed my room key into the girl on reception before standing outside the hotel. Jack was already outside and was already halfway through a cigarette. I was just about to talk to him when Tracey turned up nearby. I walked over to her car as she got out.

'So, the holiday is over is it?' she asked as she looked at the waiting coach which was still having cases loaded into it.

'Yes,' I sighed, 'it's been a good holiday.'

'It certainly has,' Tracey replied. 'I've met someone who I hope to be with for a long time and had a great time with.'

'I'm hoping that's me,' I returned.

'No,' said Tracey with a hint of sarcasm. 'I found a manager for my solo career!'

I must have looked disappointed as she said that as Tracey quickly revealed that she was indeed talking about me and was having a laugh. Jack found the joke more amusing than me and laughed before turning his back on us to light another cigarette away from the wind that was blowing steadily. As he did so I heard him whisper, 'What a twat!'

'You're talking as if you've been on holiday as well even though you live around here!' I said continuing the conversation..

'I am aren't I?' she said with a giggle. She then wiped a tear from her eye.

'I only came here to play a couple of gigs and to have a break from my normal day job but it's turned out to be something much more enjoyable. I'm hoping that we'll stay together after this holiday is finished even though we live so far apart.'

'We'll still be together,' I replied hugging her 'no amount of distance can keep me away from you!'

Jack then interrupted. 'Shall I order a double bed for you two lovers or have you already got one?'

'We've already got one thanks,' Tracey replied sarcastically, 'but you can buy us a box of condoms if you prefer!'

'Which sort?' Jack said, seemingly enjoying the game of sarcasm tennis.

'The ribbed ones for added pleasure,' replied Tracey.

'Oh, that reminds me,' Jack then said, 'I placed last night's dobber underneath my bed in the hotel room before I vacated it. I'd love to see the face of whoever cleans out the room!'

'Do you enjoy leaving little gifts for people you don't even know?' I asked.

'Yep,' Jack grinned, 'I've even left a bloody handprint on the wall behind the chest of drawers. I brought a small bottle of fake blood from that joke shop, covered my hands in it and then slapped them on the wall before running my hands downwards. It looks like it's the final message from a person who has been horribly murdered! If anybody finds that they will go batshit crazy!'

Me and Tracey then made a few final plans. She agreed to drive to the service station and stay with me a little longer until my coach taking me back to where I live, arrived. She also agreed to put all of my hand luggage which amounted to four bags into her car so that I wouldn't have to mess around with taking them onto the coach with me and then take them back off and keep them with me at the service station while I waited for the final coach. Tracey then asked if the coach was going straight to the service station.

'Not a chance!' I retorted, 'It will most likely take a detour around several villages and even stop off at another smaller service station for a quick break before departing for the main service station.'

'Well, let me know if the coach does that and I'll see if I can meet you there as well.'

The porters had finished packing all of the cases onto the coach and all of the elderly guests who had not yet got onto the coach boarded. Jack and I were the last to get onto the coach mainly because we both said goodbye to our respective partners first. Jenny had turned up some time after Tracey had and was even more of an emotional wreck than her bandmate was. As I understood it she was also going to meet Jack at the service station but whereas I was going to get onto the feeder coach to go back home she was actually going to taxi her other half straight to his house. Tracey suspected why this was and it wasn't normally something that could have been discussed in the restaurant at breakfast! Moments after I had sat down in my seat the coach door closed and the engine roared into life.

A familiar belch echoed over the tannoy in the coach before the driver spoke.

'Did you all enjoy your holiday?' he asked which was followed up by a mixed reception of moans and cheers.

'Did you all enjoy the lovely hotel and its entertainment?' was his second question which was followed by the same mixed reception of moans and cheers.

'Was there anything you particularly liked about the holiday?' the driver asked.

'The girls on the reception were babes!' Jack shouted in reply.

'Yes... well... enough of all of this,' said the driver as if embarrassed with Jack's answer. 'Our destination is Crappy Services but because we aren't due to arrive there until 3pm we will take a wonderful journey through some of this area's scenic villages before stopping at the peaceful Mossy Garden Centre for half an hour where we can get something to eat in their restaurant and also have a browse around their lovely large garden centre. When we return to the coach we will be on the road for another hour and then we'll stop for a forty-five minute break at a nearby shopping centre and service station. Here you will be able to visit some of the lovely shops in the shopping centre and also maybe pick up something to eat again.'

'Hang on,' shouted Jack, 'if we aren't due at the service station until 3pm why have you picked us up at the holiday resort at the crack of dawn? We could have had a few extra hours there instead of visiting some rubbish garden centre and a shopping precinct!'

'Because,' retorted the driver, 'every guest has to be out of the hotel in the morning so that they could prepare the rooms for the next guests.'

'If that was the case,' said Jack, 'we could have chucked our luggage on the coach and left it there until we could depart in the afternoon. I would have preferred a few extra hours on holiday than having to walk around a bleeding garden centre for half an hour!'

I smiled at this reply. Jack was certainly right and a few extra hours in Claptout-by-the-Sea would have been much better but I suspected he only wanted a few extra hours there so that he could give Jenny's bed another test of its agility! The driver then came back with his reply.

'Insurance reasons I'm afraid,' replied the driver before belching which was his way of signalling that the discussion was over.

After driving through various small villages where we again had a few near misses with parked cars and also driving past several turn-offs that pointed to Crappy Services we eventually stopped at Mossy Garden Centre. I had texted Tracey a short while earlier and she agreed to meet me at the garden centre which she duly did. She had beaten the coach to the garden centre despite the coach having a head start over her! I got off the coach through the side door and went to meet her where she was standing in front of her parked car nearby.

'This is a different place to Claptout-by-the-Sea isn't it,' she said, 'I haven't been here since I was a child. My mother took me here to get a Christmas tree one year and we walked out with one that died on us about five days before Christmas Day and we had to get rid of it because it looked like a bunch of twigs in a plant pot! We never went to this place again!'

Together we walked around the garden centre which was full of the usual flora and fauna I expected from such a place before having a quick bite to eat in the restaurant. Mr and Mrs Stopwatch were already there and we both watched them expecting them to find some problem with the food.

We weren't disappointed!

As the elderly couple stormed out of the restaurant amid the surprised restaurant staff we both sat down to eat. We had ordered a cheese and ham toasted sandwich each and found it to be acceptable for this kind of place but not overly enjoyable. As we left the restaurant we noticed a couple arguing with a member of staff in the main garden centre itself. We inched a little closer to eavesdrop!

'I brought this plant yesterday and look at it now — its

dead!' said a young man who looked a bit like Nigel Mansell to a bemused member of staff who looked like the kind of American high school nerd complete with black rimmed glasses held together with tape. The customer was holding out a plant that looked like it had been treated with the same kind of respect as the end of a cigarette when its smoker held a lit match up to it.

'Have you got a receipt for the purchase?' said the assistant who also sounded like an American high school nerd.

'Of course I haven't,' replied Mansell, 'when I brought the plant from you I didn't expect a problem.'

'Did you keep it watered properly?' asked the nerd.

'The instructions didn't tell me to,' replied Mansell.

'Plants don't come with instructions because it's assumed that the buyer knows how to feed and water it properly.'

'I got instructions with it but it didn't tell me to feed or water it so I didn't!'

'What did the instructions say?' asked the nerd.

'It just told me the name of the plant and a picture of it sitting in a plant pot in the middle of a sunny garden. Because the picture on boxes of frozen food are normally considered to be serving suggestions I assumed that this picture was an instruction on how to look after it!'

'So what did you do?'

'I put it in a plant incubator and turned the heat up to max to simulate the sunny conditions in the picture because it was raining when I got the plant home.'

'There's your answer then,' said the nerd, 'you killed it by subjecting it to extreme heat. You can't get a refund now!'

'You bastard!' spat Mansell before walking off and throwing the dead plant onto the floor of the garden centre.

After this debacle me and Tracey took a quick walk

through the garden centre just to make us look like people who were genuinely here to buy something and not a couple who have been dropped off by a holiday coach driver who couldn't be bothered to take us to the service station at an acceptable time. After watching somebody's pet dog urinate up the side of a large potted plant standing on the ground we noticed Jack seemingly having a row with a different member of staff but who shared the same nerd-like features as the first one. He was holding a large framed painting of a grotesque-looking dog sitting next to an equally grotesque looking pig and was showing the assistant his bloodied right hand. I caught some of the conversation and it appeared that he had cut his hand on the picture whilst holding it and wanted to see the manager to complain. After a short while the manager arrived and, after a short discussion, Jack accepted the picture as compensation for the injury caused. As he walked away he noticed me and walked over to where I stood.

'It's amazing what fake blood and a fake stick-on injury can do,' he grinned!

The half hour was soon up and I boarded the coach while Tracey drove to our next port of call. Before we parted once more she did ask why I didn't just travel with her instead of my preferred method of travelling by coach.

'The coach driver always does a headcount before leaving,' I replied, 'besides, the coach has my case.'

'I'm sure you could arrange it with the driver to finish off the journey with me. My car can hold your case easily.'

There was no doubt I was beaten. It would actually be more pleasurable to travel with Tracey but I really wanted to experience the 'joy' of a coach holiday. It isn't a coach holiday if you're travelling by car!

'Each to their own!' said Tracey shrugging.

Chapter 17
The Last Leg

We were on the road for a further hour before we stopped at the promised shopping centre. When I got off the coach I looked around for Tracey but I couldn't find her. I sat on an outdoor bench near a bus shelter and waited but still nothing. I texted her but got no reply which was when I became worried that my refusal to travel with her might have put her in a bad mood with me. I toyed with the idea that she had fallen out with me and my bags full of holiday stuff and my own hand luggage bag containing toiletries and other smaller essential items had been dumped by the roadside somewhere. Surely this wasn't the case and there had to be a perfectly reasonable explanation for her absence. I stood up and walked into the large four storey shopping centre and purchased a drink and a sandwich which were both expensive but didn't surprise me considering that this was nothing more than a glorified service station out in the middle of nowhere. I texted Tracey again but got no reply for a second time and now I was convinced that she had fallen out with me.

The sight of Mr and Mrs Sneer walking out of a superstore with another bag of shopping didn't raise my hopes and even the arrival of Jack failed to being me much hope. The minutes ticked by and a third text message went unanswered as did an actual phone call.

'Never mind,' said Jack in his usual way, after I had told him 'women will always be women. Don't expect them to be the kind of lovey-dovey babes that hang off your shoulder swooning at you promising you the world!'

'But I never expected this to happen. Besides, she's got all of my holiday trinkets!'

'So what?' replied Jack. 'All you've ever brought is a load of crappy fridge magnets and pens and pencils! They're not exactly family heirlooms are they!'

The forty-five minutes was soon up and we boarded the coach once more. Jack sat in his normal seat but the adjoining seat was taken up by the large bizarre picture. From what he was telling me he wanted this picture specifically so that he could cause some kind of reaction with the other coach passengers. He had succeeded there as Mr and Mrs Stopwatch was tutting and saying things along the lines of 'nasty looking picture' and 'a disgrace to the world of art!' I was by this point feeling bad. As the coach drove off I just wanted this holiday to be over. This had put a massive dent in my excitement and everything I had enjoyed with Tracey this week now meant nothing to me. A further hour on the road later and something out of the blue happened. Jack walked down the coach to sit next to me to bring me some news.

'Jenny's just texted me,' he said, 'Tracey has phoned her from a public phone box to tell her to tell you that she was stuck in traffic and her phones battery had gone flat! It took her ages to find a public phone box apparently but she says she will meet up with you at Crappy Services when you reach it.' This lifted my spirits a lot and suddenly all of my negative thoughts vanished within moments.

'So she hasn't fallen out with me then?' I said to Jack.

'Nope,' he replied, 'it's a good job that I'm porking one of her mates otherwise you wouldn't have known this!'

Crappy Services arrived about an hour or so after Jack had told me the news and as we pulled into the service station I could see Tracey parked up in a nearby car park with her standing by the side of her car watching the coaches arrive and depart. I got off the coach and walked briskly towards Tracey who threw her arms around me when I was close enough.

'I'm sorry about not meeting you at the shopping centre,' she said apologetically, 'how can I make it up to you?'

'You don't need to,' I said, 'Jack explained everything to me. It wasn't your fault why you were held up.'

'It's quite fortunate that Jenny is dating Jack isn't it?'

'Dating?' I said curiously. 'Is that what you call it?'

'Why? What do you call it?' Tracey asked quizzically.

'Let's just say that the word begins with 'F' and leave it at that!'

Tracey laughed as she realised what I meant.

As the luggage from all of the coaches were removed and then sorted out into separate piles to go onto other coaches I watched Jenny turn up and Jack get into the car with his luggage. We were planning to walk over to them and say goodbye but as soon as their faces locked together we thought better. Instead we walked into the main building of Crappy Services where all of the shops and cafes were. It was to be at least an hour before my feeder coach would arrive so Tracey and I stopped for a bite to eat at the same restaurant I had had breakfast at a week earlier before browsing some of the overpriced items in the shops.

The meal we had was underwhelming at best and not worth the money we paid for it. The shops offered very little we wanted to buy but we did notice Mr and Mrs Sneer standing reading a gardening magazine each.

'Do you think they'll buy the magazines they're reading?' asked Tracey in a whisper so as the Sneers wouldn't hear her.

'Not a chance,' I whispered back, 'they most likely read magazines in newsagents all the while and never buy them. I bet they've got all of their gardening knowledge from

174

magazines they have read but never brought over the years!'

We watched a little longer as Mr Sneer pointed out a feature to his wife in his magazine which she quickly read and nodded in approval before doing the same likewise. Mr Sneer also nodded positively and then they both put their magazines back on the rack and reached for another one each. Feeling that I needed to buy something from the shop so as not to look like the Sneers, I purchased a cheap puzzle book and a bottle of water and left the outlet. Tracey and I then sat on a bench facing the entrance of the shop and watched as the Sneers put their second magazine back on the rack and reached for a third one each!

Half an hour later an electronic display sign notified all of the Golden Trip coach passengers which feeder coach they would be travelling back home on and when it would depart. It appeared that we would have another thirty-five minutes together here at Crappy Services so we walked outside and had a gentle stroll around the area which was about as scenic as a walk through a petrol station! Nearby was a hotel called The Crappy Hotel and across the road was indeed a petrol station. Not far into the distance were a few houses which made me wonder who would live in a place that was so close to a service station where coaches and trucks pulled in regularly. As we walked around the service station I noticed a man in his late forties or early fifties wearing a T-shirt saying, 'I went to Muddy Beach' accompanied by a picture of a beach that looked like a football pitch during the rainy season after it had already been used for a game. We then noticed Everage and Norden sitting down on a nearby patch of grass eating homemade sandwiches and brandishing a Thermos flask. Jenny and Jack had already left and in just over half an hour so would Tracey. She wouldn't be accompanying me back to my house but rather going back to her own place. We would be speaking to each other on the phone regularly however and she did promise to visit me at my house a couple of days after I had got back home.

The time soon ebbed away and my feeder coach was ready to take on passengers. I kissed Tracey goodbye and held hands for as long as we could as if we were in some cheap romance movie before I boarded the coach with my bags full of holiday trinkets Tracey had taken out of her car. I got on the coach and looked at Tracey standing there looking sad and waving goodbye to me. The coach driver then took a headcount and closed the doors before starting the engines. As the coach drew off I waved goodbye to a clearly tearful Tracey before settling down in my seat. As the service station disappeared from view I thought about the week I had had and all of the wonderful things I had experienced.

After taking a taxi back home I got through the door of my house dumped my case and all of my hand luggage on the floor of the lounge before slumping down on the sofa. I must have slept for an hour before awaking and picking up a week's worth of bills and junk mail off the doormat. The bills I opened and quickly read while the junk mail I tore vertically in half before depositing them in the kitchen bin. I then searched through my bags of hand luggage and was surprised to find a folded up poster in one of them. I opened it up and it was a poster advertising the gig at the Punk Establishment where I had first seen The Six Pissed Dolls. On the back there was message.

'I may be a punk chick but I'm also a softy sometimes. Don't ever leave me I love you! Kisses — Tracey.'

The message was ended with a lipstick kiss.

I smiled and stored the poster in a safe place where it couldn't get damaged before unpacking.

Epilogue

Tracey and I walked hand-in-hand down the seafront of Claptout-by-the-Sea. It had been a little over nine months since the original holiday here had ended and several things had changed. My workplace had closed down and I had been made redundant so with the pitiful money I had been paid I decided to move down to the coast to be closer to Tracey. We had moved in together almost immediately and we were only just starting to settle down after all of the work we had put into making the house look like something we would be comfortable in.

Golden Trip Coaches no longer did holidays to Claptout-by-the-Sea due to the sterling work of Mr and Mrs Stopwatch. Their son had gone to great lengths to report on all of the negative points the elderly couple had told him and this damaged the reputation of Golden Trip Coaches. Pratt's had picked up the contract left by their rival coach firm and now they took holidaymakers to the Hotel Claptout where suddenly it was seemingly a hotel to enjoy your stay in! The Six Pissed Dolls had also split up during this time and Tracey had launched her solo career with the help of fellow bandmate Katie who had helped her write a few new songs. Tracey was now a regular at George Brewer's place The Brewer's Bar and everybody seemed to like her. The other members of the band were also doing other things including Jenny who, following the bands break-up, had moved down into Jack's part of the country and that was the last either of us had heard of her.

Both of us lived in a small house in an equally small

village called Little Sense which was only about a mile away from Claptout-by-the-Sea. The house now felt like our own although you wouldn't have thought it after I had shipped all of my fridge magnets and little models acquired from various holidays over the years into there! Tracey didn't mind a few fridge magnets but she wasn't exactly a fan of three-hundred plus fridge magnets I had in my possession. Therefore, we had come to a compromise and ten of my most favourite fridge magnets went on the door of the fridge while the rest were displayed on a large metal notice board stuck to the wall of my study where books and guides of various holiday resorts also resided.

Claptout-by-the-Sea had become almost a daily favourite with us due to its closeness to home. When I wasn't working I was walking along the seafront enjoying the sea air as well as the bizarre characters that resided on the beach. I had managed to get a job working in a factory in the nearby town of Chipshop (which was pronounced Chips-hop to anybody not familiar with these kind of place names). Surprisingly I had gathered a few interesting facts and answers to questions when I started at the factory. The workplace was none other than the day job of the person who had been nicknamed 'Pube-like' and I had replaced the mouthy person who had coined the name. The person in question was also a person of some interest to me. I had discovered that my predecessor was none other than the illustrious KFC Kid and, according to his now former workmates the initials stood for 'Knighthood For Clarkson' because barely a day passed when he wasn't talking about the pressing matter of TV presenter Jeremy Clarkson not yet receiving a knighthood! It had become something of an annoying topic of conversation for his workmates both in the factory where I currently worked and also at least one of his previous jobs and the punch he received after getting off the tour bus several months ago wasn't the first he had received or even the last! He had originally come from the same area of the country as me which would explain why his graffiti also appeared around there.

Tracey also had a day job as she had before I had met her and it was just fortunate that she was on a week's holiday from work when I had bumped into her at Rusty Pier all those months ago. If she had been at work on that week, we might never have met — or at least we would only have set eyes on each other during her gig at The Punk Establishment. Tracey is adamant it was all down to fate and that there was some higher power who brought us together on that week. Myself? I just think it was just a coincidence! I only came here for a week away and to buy a few fridge magnets!

I still hadn't got over my fear of going on the Ferris wheel but I also hadn't lost my enthusiasm for going on one either so that is why I shakily stepped onto Claptout-by-the-Sea's Ferris wheel one more time. As Tracey enjoyed the ascent I closed my eyes but all I could think of was images of the little boy from the previous holiday who was now climbing up the gantry of the Ferris wheel with a spanner in his hand laughing as he reached my bucket! I opened my eyes just as the kid began to unscrew the first bolt and returned to reality. I hugged Tracey more as a form of protection but also to show my love for her. After the Ferris wheel had finished I walked off with legs that were shaking around like Elvis Presley and sat down on the nearby bench I had first found when I originally got off the ride. After catching my breath, I stood up and walked further along the seafront with Tracey.

After a short walk we decided to savour the delights of Claptout-by-the-Sea's dungeon amusement. We had both promised to check it out when I was last on holiday here but other things seemed to take precedence. Despite Tracey living in this area for some time she had never visited the dungeon and so we were both 'newbies' to the attraction. Sitting in a little kiosk just inside the doorway was a bloke about the same age as me wearing a ghastly tank top and looking like he didn't want to be there. As he asked for the eight pounds admission fee each his tone of voice echoed that sentiment. He then pointed us to a doorway shrouded in a long black curtain and we stepped through. We stood there for about a minute before somebody approached us. The man in the tank top stood in front of us and announced that he would be our guide for the walk-through attraction which disappointed us both. We expected a near-frightening character to be our guide but the only frightening thing about him was his choice of fashion! It was therefore quite relieving then that he was suddenly ambushed by a character actor wearing a cheap plastic hockey mask and brandishing an equally cheap-looking plastic toy chainsaw to 'bump off' the guide. As the chainsaw maniac made whirring sounds with his mouth (because the toy didn't have any sound effects of its own) the tank top wearing guide dropped to the floor and tried to convince us that he had been chopped into pieces when it was quite visibly obvious due to the candlelit lamps on the various walls that he crawled 'off set' and through a side door which most likely led back to the kiosk. The chainsaw maniac then gave chase and we ran pretending to be petrified around the maze of corridors which included blood-stained hospital walls and algae-covered brick dungeon walls amid screams of terror from presumably other characters who were being dissected. When the attraction was over the final door lead us into a gift shop where I brought a pen, pencil and fridge magnet which caused Tracey to sigh and tut as she walked towards the cash till with me.

We then walked towards Rusty Pier and standing outside of the pier was a bloke dressed as the pier's mascot complete with combat fatigues and a plastic machine gun. The gun he was holding appeared to be attached to the costumes hands and I laughed as the strange meerkat figure frightened off a few young kids by suddenly turning around and pointing the gun at their faces! Just when I thought it couldn't get any more entertaining one kid was frightened off by the mascot and his father went on the offensive by giving the meerkat a left hook across the face which sent him falling to the ground. As his child cried he grabbed the bloke in the meerkat costume by the throat and almost throttled him until a security guard at the pier broke them away. After the altercation we walked along the pier and were amazed to find that Bertie Dastard was performing there tonight.

'Do you remember him?' Tracey smiled.

'I certainly do,' I replied, 'it was where we first got talking.'

'Do you fancy going to see him tonight?' she then suggested.

'I'd love to,' I replied.

'There's a live band playing at George's place tonight as well.'

'Really?' I said, 'are they any good?'

'Not unless you like reggae music. They're a British band called P45 and apparently they're not too bad.'

'I'm not into reggae that much,' I said, 'I still think that seeing Bertie would be better.'

'Me too,' smiled Tracey.

As we walked along the pier Tracey then looked at me.

'I have something to tell you,' she said with a straight face.

'What is it,' I said.

'I'm pregnant,' she replied.

Printed in Great Britain
by Amazon